FOLLOW

By Rusty Moore

TABLE OF CONTENTS

CHAPTER I

The Crossover

The car slowed as Tim Louden pulled it off the road onto the shoulder. He stopped the car just short of a sharp curve in the road. Which, in the pale moonlight, made it look like the road ended there. The night was dead calm with no breeze, which made the night air feel heavy. Lisa Riley breathed in the night air as she closed the car door. Lisa could smell the woods as she walked toward the front of the car; she could smell the hot metal of the car engine, and she could smell Tim as they came together in front of the car.

"Well, now what?" Lisa asked as they leaned on the hood of the car.

"Now we wait," Tim said with half a smile.

As they stood there, Lisa was anxious about what she had gotten herself into. Her thoughts went back to when she and Tim had first met. That moment had set forth all the weird events leading up to this night.

Lisa was a bartender at a pub in downtown Hendersonville, Tennessee. She was a slender, pretty woman with long blonde hair, strong legs and arms from working so many shifts behind the bar. Her wit had been chiseled to a fine point, and she could hold her own with any of the local men who wanted to try their jokes with her. In fact, some tried her just to hear her comebacks, and she had sent many a man home with his tail between his legs. She was working the night Tim came running into the place and slid very quickly up to the bar, where he grabbed someone else's drink and was drinking it when the police came busting in and slowly walked through the bar. No one said anything to the police, and they left shaking their heads. Lisa knew Tim was in some sort of trouble, and that drew her to him. He was tall, dark, and handsome, and those three things also caught her eye. She was fixed on Tim for the rest of the night. Looking back, Lisa is not sure if Tim stayed till closing that night because of her attention or because the police kept moving around outside. It did not matter anyway since it had been six months now, and they had been together since that night. The things Tim told her were almost too unreal to believe, with an alternate world taking our dead souls and reviving them to rebuild a realm. That was Tim's version of what was going on. Looking through Tim's special lens into the night and seeing wavy blue portals way in the distance. Hendersonville apparently being an epicenter for the portals. The portals themselves sounded scary, a blue shadow sphere of light. That could only be seen through a special lens of some sort. Jewelry and precious stones just waiting to be taken from the other side; it was all quite intriguing. That's what brought her here tonight to see just what Tim was talking about.

Lisa was startled back into reality by Tim touching her hand. He was looking through what looked like one of those old view master things. She looked up fast and saw him motioning with his eyes to the far side of the road. Lisa took the viewer and looked through it in the direction Tim was pointing. What Lisa saw made her gasp a little and sent a chill over her. There was a very thin man standing there. His clothes were old, faded, and dirty. He looked like he had been living on the streets for a long time. He stood there for what seemed like an hour, though, at that moment Lisa had no perception of time. Finally, this thin, ragged man began to move across the road. Move was not the right word; float wasn't even the right word. The man moved as if being dragged by some unknown force. His feet were jerking along the surface of the road he was writhing as if it hurt him to move. As he passed directly in front of Lisa, she realized she could dimly see through him like a ghost. The ragged man looked straight at Lisa, and their eyes met. It made Lisa think of having a bad dream where you are about to be killed, or you are falling, and you can't stop it or scream, you feel paralyzed with fear. The man opened his mouth wide as if he was screaming, but there was no sound. Then Lisa noticed a gentle rustle in the trees like the wind makes. Was that his scream? Lisa thought as the man got to the other side of the road, Tim took the viewer from Lisa and grabbed Lisa's hand, and they started following the ragged man.

"We have to keep up," Tim said hurriedly as they left the road and started into the woods. As they went further into the woods, Tim kept looking back and forth into the viewer and at where he was going while getting closer and closer to the ragged man.

"There it is," Tim yelled as he looked through the viewfinder.

Lisa was following Tim as closely as she could. As they drew near, the blue sphere, Tim started to crouch down as he was walking fast, and Lisa started crouching too.

"What's on the other side?" Lisa yelled.

"Not sure never been there," Tim yelled back as he was fighting through brush and briars.

His answer made Lisa realize Tim had never talked about the other side, other than riches and treasure. She had just assumed he knew what he was getting them into. Now though, as they were about to go to the other side, Lisa was suddenly unsure of her boyfriend and terrified.

The ragged man was pulled into the light, his body twisting and writhing as he went into it.

"Come on," Tim said as he bent down and went into the dim light. Lisa followed without hesitation because she trusted Tim, though her mind was screaming not to go into the light, she was having serious second thoughts. She pushed on through the portal, clutching Tim's hand.

Once they were through the sphere, Lisa realized quickly that they had entered some sort of alternate reality. Tim handed Lisa the viewer, and she looked through it at the old, ragged man. The ragged man was no longer ragged. He was a young man and was walking very easily now as he walked away from them, and he walked with a purpose. Lisa thought for an instant. Where is he going? She handed the viewer back to Tim and took a long look around, and they were still in some woods, but the trees were small and seemed to be twisted and were just silhouettes of trees. It was daylight here, though there was no sun in the sky. What was that smell? Lisa thought as she stood there, taking in all the changes in this new world. It was a horrid odor like burning trash, and it did not go away. Every breath Lisa took had a putrid smell. Tim took Lisa's hand, and they started making their way back the way they had come toward his car. She quickly realized the car, the road, everything in the world she knew was gone. After only a few steps, Tim stopped, bent down, and picked up a band-type ring lying on the ground. He stuck it in his backpack. He stopped several more times and gathered up some rings and a watch. A few minutes later, they came to town. The town seemed to be coming at them as they were going toward it. However, this town was old and not just run down; it was decaying like a dead log in the forest. The buildings and structures looked oddly familiar, though. As they walked down the street, Lisa realized this was her town, this was Hendersonville. Yes, there was the bar where she worked or at least the shell of the building, the stores she shopped in, but the doors and windows were gone. The buildings were crumbling; the sidewalks and streets were being swallowed by the weeds and overgrowth. Lisa's head was spinning as she bumped into Tim, who had stopped and was bent down picking up jewels in front of what looked like a bank. Lisa was trying to get all her senses in check so she could close her mouth and stop wondering in awe.

"Come on!" Tim seemed to yell as he took off into the crumbling structure that was once the bank.

"Wait!" was all Lisa could muster as she took off toward Tim.

Once inside the bank, Tim went straight down to the floor and started grabbing handfuls of jewelry. The stuff was everywhere; some of the diamonds actually sparkled a little, the way they did on the store shelves back in the real world. A world Lisa was really starting to miss. Tim grabbed his backpack and began shoving jewels inside. There seemed to be rings and necklaces all over the floor. He filled his backpack until it was all he could carry, grabbed several more pieces and stuck them in his pockets. Lisa was just standing there, still taking all of this in, not knowing or even thinking about what was to come next.

"Let's go." Tim snapped as he put his backpack on his back and headed for the door. Lisa was just blindly following him at this point because that was the only command she could get her brain to process. They hurried back out into the street, where Tim looked both ways, then started in the same direction they had been going. Lisa noticed several pieces of jewels on the ground as they went by, but she was too scared to stop and pick any up, afraid she would lose Tim and be lost here forever. Shortly, they were heading back into the woods, which looked like the place where they had followed the old man through, but she couldn't be sure. As they approached the stained bricks and broken concrete of the town's edge, Tim stopped and started looking all around through the viewer.

"Now we wait." Tim said with a small grin, putting the viewer up to his eyes.

"Wait, wait for what?" Lisa said, still unsure of where she was or what she was doing.

"Wait for another portal," Tim said as he turned his head, trying to look through the viewer in every direction.

As they stood there waiting, Lisa took the opportunity to look back at the town they had just come from. The sights and smells were beyond anything she could have ever imagined. For a moment, she felt anger toward Tim for bringing her here. Her mind started racing. What if they couldn't back through the portal? What if they couldn't find a portal? Lisa found herself staring at Tim, hoping, praying he could get her back into her world. It did not take long before another sphere of light appeared close to the ground. Tim took off toward the light, but before he could get there, he realized Lisa wasn't right behind him. When he looked through the viewer, the light was gone, and another person headed off toward the lights of the distant town. Lisa realized she was still standing where she was. She jerked herself back to reality and ran toward Tim.

"Ok, listen," Tim said with a real sense of urgency in his voice.

"To get back, we have to move through the light, together in the opposite direction they are coming through." Time explained.

"Get ready, when I say go, do not hesitate, just follow me as closely as you can." Tim finished his instructions while looking all around through the viewer intensely.

Lisa was so scared at this moment, her heart was pounding, and every fiber in her brain focused on Tim as he searched for a glowing gateway. Lisa wondered what would happen if they couldn't find another portal or if Tim got through and she didn't. Just as her mind was starting to go into a full panic, she heard Tim.

"Now!" Tim shouted as he rushed toward a new gate. Lisa was right beside him this time and lurched forward as well. As Lisa passed through the portal, she also passed through the woman coming the other way. It was like feeling the mist of light rain or heavy fog on her skin. For just an instant, she felt the power of whatever was pulling the woman pull on her. Lisa pushed forward with all her might and came out onto the other side of the portal with such force that her legs could not keep up with her momentum, and she went tumbling across a sidewalk. Tim grabbed her by her arm and pulled her up.

"Run" was all he said.

As Lisa was running, she was collecting her thoughts and getting a grip on what was going on around her. She followed Tim to a spot on a street in between two parked cars, where they crouched down.

Where are we?" Lisa whispered.

"I'm not sure." Tim said as he peeked up over the cars where they were hiding.

"We need to hide the backpack and then figure it out." Tim said.

Tim checked his watch; it was two thirty in the morning. Lisa thought it was weird that they had gone into the portal a little after eleven o'clock. They were only over there for a few minutes, but three and a half hours had gone by. Tim shoved the backpack up under the car as far as he could, then stood up. He reached down and pulled Lisa up. They started walking down the street, trying to look like a normal couple. As they walked, they were looking for a clue as to where they were. Nothing looked familiar, and then they saw a sign over a hotel that said, Glenrock Hotel.

"Where the hell is Glenrock?" Lisa snapped. Tim had his phone out and was already searching for the town.

"Wyoming." Tim said, looking straight at Lisa.

"At least we are still in the United States." Tim said smiling.

"Stay here, do not move, and wait till I get back." Tim was walking away as he finished his instructions.

Tim took off walking as fast as he could without raising suspicion. He went back to the parked cars and grabbed his backpack, then hurried back to Lisa. They went inside the hotel, and Tim used his credit card to check in. Once in their room, Tim poured all the jewels he had collected out on the bed. Lisa sat down on the edge of the bed with a thump and sat there thinking about what had just happened. She didn't care about all the jewels; she was just glad to be back in this world. She didn't know whether to cry or dance. Tim clumsily fumbled through the jewels, holding several pieces up to the light and smiling.

"We should be able to get a lot of money for this." Tim said as he hugged and kissed Lisa, and they collapsed on the bed and fell asleep.

Early the next morning, Tim went to get a car so they could head back to Hendersonville, Tennessee, which seemed a world away.

The drive was long, and Lisa's mind was racing through a long list of questions. She did not have answers to yet.

"How did you get involved in this whole thing?" Lisa asked. Tim slowly turned his head and looked at Lisa for several seconds.

"The company approached me." Tim said. "I am a hometown guy born and raised in Hendersonville, so I got in at a higher level than most of the other followers." Tim talked without taking his eyes off the road.

"Once they explained how the whole thing works, I started building my own plan. Never been much of a follower, I guess." Tim chuckled as he finished.

"So, it's just run back and forth through those portals and grab as much as you can?" Lisa asked.

"Pretty much, or at least that's my plan." Tim said.

The company has some notion of keeping someone over there and letting them direct the crossers and followers so they can get even more. I even heard them talking about controlling the souls or some weird crap like that. But I say run in and grab what you can and run out." Tim was looking at Lisa now as he talked.

"They wanted me to be the first guy to stay over there. That's how I got the viewer to see the portals. But, as soon as I got that viewer, I was gone, I don't need the company or Henry telling me what to do." Tim finished talking and put his focus back on the road. The rest of the ride was quiet as Lisa was trying to figure out what the hell was going on.

Once back in Hendersonville, Tim dropped Lisa off at her place and drove on without even saying goodbye. Lisa just wanted to rest and went inside her apartment.

Later that evening, Lisa went over to Tim's apartment to check on him and see just how many jewels they had gotten. Tim didn't answer the door when she knocked, so she just let herself in. Walking through the small kitchen into the bedroom, she could feel that something was not right. When she got to the bedroom, Tim wasn't there. As she walked back into the kitchen, she saw Tim sitting on the ground just outside the back door with his head hanging down in an unnatural way. Lisa burst through the back door.

"Tim?" She spoke.

"Tim, what is it? What's wrong?" Lisa asked in a worried voice.

"I don't know, something is not right, I... feel paralyzed like I can't move." Tim said, unable to raise his head.

Lisa stood there in the backyard, frozen, just staring at Tim. She was suddenly aware of the low rustle of the wind in the trees, like she had heard the night before in the woods. But they were in Tim's backyard now. Lisa grabbed the viewer that was lying beside Tim and started looking all around the yard. She was startled by one of the souls appearing in the viewer. Lisa stood there watching through the viewer as one of those hollow bodies, energized from the other side, came up to Tim. It opened its mouth and leaned toward Tim. As it passed through Tim, he let out a small whine and fell backward onto the grass. Then his soul rose up as he turned into one of the hollow bodies being dragged to the other world for eternity. Lisa was terrified, and she started looking around the yard, praying one of the beings did not come for her. She started waving her arms madly as she ran back inside to the bedroom. She was screaming to get away, though there was nothing in the room but her. She sat in the corner, trembling and crying as she awaited her fate. As she sat there, she noticed a small book lying on Tim's bed. She crawled over and grabbed it. It was a journal. In it were the answers to the questions Lisa had. She thumbed through the small book until she found an entry from Tim. The date was the night Tim came running into her bar, the night they had met. Lisa stood and walked into the kitchen, where she sat and read Tim's entry. Tim had entered the date and time. Tim had gone to the backroad where they had been the other night. There, he tried to cross over into the other world.

Tim wrote, *"I am alone in this endeavor, the company wants me to go over and stay there to see what I can find out for them. But I know the followers never come back, so the company must be killing them while they're over there. I don't need the company now that I have the information and the viewer; I can do this myself. They are trying to kill me, so I won't crossover on my own. They think they own this other realm, but they don't own me."*

According to what he wrote, about the night he met Lisa. He waited to cross over, but as the night wore on, the portals were sparse. Tim saw one in the distance and took off toward it. Just as he started running, the company men who had been sneaking up on him turned on their lights and started to chase him. As they chased him through the woods, Tim was looking through the viewer and saw one of the souls being dragged toward the light, and he knew that was the way to get to a portal, waiting till he saw the light was too late. But now he had to lose these guys. They started shooting at Tim, which drew the police into the chase. Now the police were chasing him, and he wasn't sure about the company boys. Tim ran to town and into the bar. The last word in his journal was Lisa.

Lisa sat there trying to figure this out. Tim took the jewels, and after they made it back, the other side came for him, and he died. Lisa's mind was racing. I did not touch or take the jewels, and I am fine, Lisa thought.

"Was it taking the jewels that caused Tim's demise?" Lisa said under her breath.

"Who is the company?" Lisa said as she stood to leave.

Lisa walked back into the bedroom and found a small carry-on bag; she put all the jewels in the bag, put the viewer and Tim's journal in his backpack, and left. She carried the bag of jewels down the street to her car and threw it and the backpack in the back seat. As Lisa was getting into her car, another car pulled up in front of Tim's apartment, and four men got out. They were dressed in black, from their hats to their shoes. Three of them ran up and into the house; the other man went more slowly, looking all around. When he reached the porch, he stopped and looked straight at Lisa. Lisa realized she had stopped and was staring. The man reached up and tipped his hat at Lisa. His small smile creeped Lisa out, and she quickly jumped into the car and left. As she drove away, she was wondering if that was Henry and the company Tim had told her about.

After getting back to her apartment, Lisa began studying the journal she had taken from Tim. She entered all the details from the night they crossed over. Tim's journal dated back to just over a year ago. That's when Tim joined the company to be a follower. There was nothing to explain how this was all possible. There was an entry about how three or four people go over, and one is called the crosser, they carry the viewer, finds the portals and leads the way. The others are followers; they gather up the jewels and stones and carry them back across the portal. Tim noted that the followers never return. That must be why after he got a viewer, he decided to leave the company and go over himself. There were more entries from Tim, but just single entries with no names, dates, or details, just that they were going through on that night. It seemed they had crossed over but never returned. Lisa sat and thought about the fact that the crosser who carried the viewer crossed over several times, but the followers only went across once. She went back and reread the entries from Tim's journal.

The crosser must take someone with him, and they gather the jewels and carry them back through. The crosser never touches the jewels in the other world. Lisa suddenly realized she hadn't touched the jewels on the other side; she had been too scared to help Tim grab any.

"Death comes for those who take from the other world. So, if I don't take or touch the jewels over there, I'm safe and can cross over when I want." Lisa saying this out loud made her realize what potential this whole thing had. She also realized Tim's fatal mistake. He didn't realize the company wasn't killing the followers, the other side was taking them for stealing its riches.

The next day, Lisa took several pieces of the jewelry to a local jeweler and sold them. She made a surprising amount of money, which she stuck in her purse. Lisa left Hendersonville that day and now lives comfortably in a home she paid cash for in a beach town in Florida.

CHAPTER II

Going Back

Living in Sarasota, Florida was great. Selling all the jewels she and Tim had brought back made enough money to buy a small house and live comfortably. Her days were mostly made up of yoga classes, pottery shopping, antiquing, and walks on the beach. Her life was easy and simple, and she liked it that way. Lisa, however, had become bored and was thinking about going back into the alternate world to gather as much jewelry as she possibly could. She wasn't sure if it was the money, the excitement, or the danger that was drawing her back to cross over again. She remembered the feeling she had as she and Tim were following the ragged soul through the woods. Her body was tingling with excitement as they neared the portal. When she stood up in the other world, the sights were unworldly, but that smell. She could still smell that smell when she thought about it. She would need someone to follow her to gather and carry the jewelry back through the portal for her. In the back of her mind, she knew whoever she found to follow her would die, one soul, that was the cost of crossing over. Even with this weight on her conscience, she set about finding a boyfriend to help her. As she was setting up her online dating account, she was thinking about what she needed in a guy. Someone who was strong and athletic. Someone she could convince to follow her through a portal into an alternate world. Someone who would be willing to leap without knowing what's out there, a sports jock, she thought with a small smile.

Lisa met Ryan online, and they became close very fast. Ryan checked all the boxes she needed. He was a stocky man with thick black hair and a thick mustache. He had played football in college and now played on a local touch football team. His profile made him sound like he was so active that he never slept. After their first meetup date, they went out several times, then started dating. Lisa was trying to get Ryan to slow down, but he was moving fast into the relationship. After a month of dating, Lisa started to drop little teasers about what she had planned for them. Questions like, how would you like to be richer than you ever imagined you could be? Or have you ever thought about alternate realities, like in the comic books? Ryan would usually just laugh and try to grab her butt. Ryan seemed hell-bent on building a life with Lisa, but Lisa knew that would never happen. Lisa realized she had never felt anything like love for Ryan; he was just a business partner, a doomed business partner. Lisa was concerned about Ryan's life, as she knew if they crossed over and he gathered all the jewels, he would not survive. This weighed heavily on Lisa's mind, and she struggled trying to find a way to make this right. There wasn't a way to make it right if she did this; Ryan's death would be on her hands. Three months into their relationship, Lisa woke up during a storm in the middle of the night and sat up in bed. She sat and watched Ryan sleep. It was in that stormy late-night moment that Lisa realized some people were crossers; they led the way, and some people were followers. The followers gathered the jewels and things and carried them all back over, then paid the ultimate price for following. Lisa realized if she was going to do this, people would die, and she had to be alright with that. Then she remembered seeing the ragged old man change once she and Tim were on the other side. He became young again and walked off toward something as a new man. Her memory of that changed the way she looked at the followers. That was the thought that settled it for Lisa. Followers weren't just dying over here; they were being taken over to the other side to live on, maybe forever. Was the other side heaven, hell or something else? Lisa thought as she watched Ryan sleep. Either way, Ryan wouldn't be dying, he would be crossing over and on to bigger and better things. Lisa laid back down and fell asleep comfortably with her new thoughts on followers.

The next day, sitting by the pool, confident in their relationship and Ryan's future after crossing over. Lisa told Ryan about the portals and all the wealth they could build by going back and forth. She only told Ryan what she thought he needed to know to get him to go along with her plan. Ryan had a lot of questions. He questioned the reality of the viewer. So that night, Lisa took it out and let him look through it. All he saw was some wavy blue lights that sort of came into focus, then disappeared. Lisa showed Ryan the money she had left in her bank account from her trip with Tim. Finally, Ryan agreed to go along with Lisa, although Lisa felt like he was just patronizing her. About five months had passed since she crossed over the first time with Tim. This would be easy, she thought as she and her new boyfriend Ryan, set off for Hendersonville Tennessee. Once they were in the air on their way to Hendersonville, Ryan leaned over and asked. "Is this some sort of wild kinky sex adventure?"

"No, it's not. It's exactly what we talked about." Lisa said, smiling. Though she knew Ryan was still trying to process all of this and was waiting for a punch line or a fooled-you type ending. He will find out soon enough, Lisa thought as she leaned back and closed her eyes.

Once they landed in Hendersonville and rented a car, they toured the town where Lisa had grown up. Lisa was careful not to run into any of her old friends; she didn't think she could answer their questions. At one point, Lisa felt as if someone was watching her, but she shook the feeling off and went on. She and Ryan went to a store and bought two flexible carry-on-sized suitcases. About eleven o'clock that night, Ryan drove the car he had rented and took them out to the spot on the same dark road where this had all started for Lisa, five months ago, and they waited. Lisa took the viewer out of Tim's backpack and began scanning back and forth. She could see several blue lights appearing and disappearing in the distance, and she wondered if they were all souls being taken back into the other world. In the darkness, Ryan felt nervous and touched Lisa's hand with a smile. It didn't take long for Lisa to hear the low rustle from the wind in the trees and one of the doomed souls to come dragging by. Lisa handed Ryan the viewer and told him where to look. Ryan looked through the viewer and gasped.

"Now do you believe what I'm telling you?" Lisa asked, taking the viewer back. Ryan just nodded his head in agreement. Lisa pointed to the suitcases and nodded to Ryan. Ryan grabbed one in each hand as they started to follow the lost soul.

"No matter what, just follow me." Lisa said, looking through the viewer.

They followed the soul until Lisa saw the blue sphere. They rushed past the soul to get there first. Lisa crouched as she went through. She pulled Ryan into the alternate world, who seemed to hesitate. Ryan straightened up and looked around in disbelief and was unable to utter any words. Lisa led him back the way they had come into the scraggy woods, which quickly turned into a town that seemed to be coming at them as they were walking toward it. This was a different part of Hendersonville Lisa wasn't familiar with. Lisa gave it little thought as she and Ryan moved along the decaying street. Lisa found a building that looked like the door was open, and the two of them ran inside. Lisa instructed Ryan to grab as many jewels as he could find while she made sure no one was coming. Ryan, now realizing this was real and he was going to be rich, started looking around the floor for jewels. He found them scattered all around and, in some places, they had accumulated into small piles. Ryan shoved as much jewelry as he could into the bags they had brought there. Lisa was watching his work. Shortly, Ryan had two bags stuffed full of rings, necklaces, brooches, and watches.

Ok, follow me." Lisa said, walking out into the street.

Lisa heard what she thought was someone talking and turned with a jerk to look back at the decaying buildings.

"Must be my nerves." She whispered under her breath. Lisa was walking as fast as she could to get back into the woods so they could get out of here. Once in the woods, they stopped and waited.

"Now what?" Ryan whispered.

"Now we must go back through, so when I see a sphere, we go.

Don't hesitate, just follow me closely." Lisa said as she was looking around.

Lisa was looking back at the dim outline of the town when she saw a silhouette of someone coming out of one of the buildings and the dim light of a flashlight. Lisa was trying to figure out what she had just seen when Ryan grabbed her arm and started to run. Lisa was not ready and almost fell over. She regained her balance and stared at Ryan.

"What the hell?" She said, looking at Ryan. She glanced back at the town, and the dim lights were being pointed in their direction. That must be the company guys, Lisa thought as she turned her attention back to the woods. She started looking through the viewer for a portal again. She was becoming frantic to find a portal. She wasn't sure if it was knowing company guys were there and knew she and Ryan were there now. Maybe it was the fact that she just wants out of the place as soon as she can get out. Either way, Lisa could feel a panic starting to build in her chest. Then, there was a portal light very near to them. Lisa took off, and Ryan followed. As they got to the light, Lisa shoved Ryan and the money through the portal. Lisa leaned down and started through just as the soul was coming out. Lisa looked right into the woman's face as she passed through her. The woman looked oriental, Lisa thought as she came running back into the real world. The two just stopped and hunkered down. They were in some deep woods on a hill overlooking a small town.

"Where are we?" Ryan whispered.

"I'm not sure." Lisa snapped back.

After a minute of just breathing and calming down, the two of them started making their way down the hill toward the small town. It was hard getting through the thick foliage as they were dragging the two cases of heavy jewels and precious stones as they went. It seemed to take an hour or more to get down out of the woods. Once down the hill and out of the forest, they came to a road. They stayed on the edge of the road in case they needed to jump off as they followed the road into the small town. The quarter mile or so was a very intense walk, as they knew if they were caught, they would be imprisoned or worse. On the edge of town, they found themselves hiding behind some sort of small building. There were people walking and riding bikes on the street in front of the building. Everyone was oriental and spoke a language neither of them could understand. Lisa pulled her phone out to search for her location.

"Lanzhou China!" Lisa said as a wave of fear rushed over her.

Her mind shot back to what Tim had said that first night, "at least we're in the United States."

She now knew what that meant. Lisa stopped and made her mind settle down instead of going into sheer panic, which was what she was feeling. She was working on a plan, while Ryan was still in shock and could only stand and look around. Lisa crept around the building to look over the town below. She could see a port in the distance and came up with a plan.

They would have to sneak into this oceanside town and find a way to stow away on board one of those freighters. Hopefully, that freighter will be going to America. Lisa explained the plan to Ryan, and he agreed. It was already late in the afternoon, so they decided to wait till it was dark before they headed for the port. While they were waiting, a notion struck Lisa. They had gone into the other world last night, a little after eleven; they had been back on this side for maybe a couple of hours, and it was late afternoon. Time did not flow in parallel in the two worlds. Time spent there was more time expired here, and depending on where you came out on the planet, you could be many hours from where you started. Lisa decided to wait and put all of this in her journal later, and turned to the situation at hand for now. As darkness fell, they began sneaking down alleyways and in between houses, trying not to be seen. It took a while, but they finally made it. After getting close to the port and finding a good hiding spot to wait, Ryan headed off to get some supplies. While he was gone, Lisa watched several people get on board the ship. They were being checked off as they entered, but there were a lot of people going on board. She hoped they could fall into line and blend in as they went through. Ryan returned after several minutes with two backpacks full of food and water.

"What did that cost?" Lisa asked, knowing it wouldn't be long until she was alone in this.

"Nothing, I stole it." Ryan said, smiling. Lisa just shook her head, realizing that if he had gotten caught, they both would end up in a Chinese prison, only her stay would be a lot longer than Ryans.

Later that night, as the cargo freighter was being boarded by the last of the crew. Lisa and Ryan took advantage of the chaos of final boarding and fell in line. They snuck on board with each carrying one of the carry-on bags. The man checking in was way more interested in looking at Lisa's body than checking their names. Lisa loosened the top button on her shirt, smiled and looked as flirty as she could as they walked right past the man. Once on board, they found a place to hide out on deck, under some canvas tarps. They got as comfortable as they could and settled in for the night. The night air was cold as the hours slowly dragged by, with neither of them sleeping much at all. They didn't move around at all that first day, as there was a lot of activity with the ship just leaving port. They were afraid they would be caught. That next night, just after dark, Lisa heard the low rustling sound of wind in the trees from before.

Here now, Lisa thought as she watched Ryan begin to slumber where he was sitting, he never looked up or spoke again. He let out a sigh, and his body went limp as Lisa was sure his soul was taken off the ship. Lisa wondered if anyone had seen his soul leaving, but after several minutes, the quiet hum of the ship's engines brought everything back to normalcy. Lisa started writing everything she could think of in her journal. She would process this information later, she thought as she closed the journal and laid back to sleep.

It took seven more days for the ship to come into port at Seattle. During that time, Lisa had to stay with Ryan's body under the tarps. During that time also she worked out some of the more details in her head. Coming back through the portal could put her anywhere in the world where people live and die. This meant that time was no matter because if she came out on the other side of the planet, it could be twenty hours or more behind or ahead of when she went in. This put another level of fear into going back to the alternate world. Lisa decided that in the future she would carry a backpack with more than the viewer. She would carry her driver's license and her credit card. She would carry her passport, some cash, and things to help her get home from anywhere in the world. She would also find a good bag the size of a carry-on bag that was durable, flexible and easy to carry. This would allow for more jewels to be brought back and have them tucked neatly into a closeable bag that could be handled more easily than a regular stiff carry-on bag.

Finally, who was it she saw on the other side with the flashlight? Was it the company Tim mentioned in his journal? Lisa's mind was again racing full of thoughts and fears, but she had to get back home first.

Lisa was never so happy to be back in the United States as she was when the ship docked. Come to think of it, Lisa had never been outside the United States till now. This thought made her smile. She waited to see a line of people leaving the ship. She just fell into the line and walked right past the crew, carrying both bags. She was careful not to make eye contact or raise any suspicions. She started talking to one of the oriental ladies and laughing as they walked past the crew. The Chinese lady probably thought she was crazy and didn't understand a thing she said, but her ploy worked as they walked by the crew and off the freighter.

Once she was off the ship and away from the port, she could breathe a sigh of relief. She sat down on a street bench to relax and get her mind straight. While she was sitting there, she realized she probably had several hundred thousand dollars in these two carry-on bags in jewels and precious stones just sitting here in the open.

Lisa thought about getting plane tickets to get home as fast as possible.

No, I can't get these bags of jewels through the airport; I'll have to drive. Lisa thought to herself as she got up and started walking down the street.

She made her way to a hotel and checked in, using her credit card. After a night of rest in the hotel room, Lisa rented a car. She headed for Florida. It's about a three-day drive if she drives straight through. Lisa set out not knowing how far she would be able to get. The drive was long, and she stopped in East Texas to get some sleep. As Lisa laid down to sleep, she felt a tinge of guilt over using Ryan the way she did, but it passed quickly as she remembered he was alive and well on the other side. Then she started wondering about the company and how she was going to stay ahead of them.

The next night, Lisa made it home to Sarasota and let herself in. It was very late, and she fell into her bed and slept way into the next day. When she did get up, she took a long, hot shower, washing the last ten or so days off in the shower. Lisa spent the rest of the afternoon going through the jewels and things she had brought back. She separated the jewels into categories like rings, bracelets and necklaces, and all the other things. She put it all in containers in the closet.

"I'm sorry Ryan." Lisa said as she closed the closet doors.

Lisa took time to figure out how to sell all the jewels without raising attention to herself. She took small batches to several jewelers and pawn shops. Over the course of about a month, Lisa made more than five hundred thousand dollars, which she quickly put into her bank account.

Living in Florida and doing whatever she likes each day makes her happy, and she doesn't think too much about her secret. Life is good for her, though she does get bored, as life on this side of the grave is mundane and tedious. It's not long until she is letting her mind wander about going back over, and she realizes going across is the only thing that excites her. So, if she has people to follow her, Lisa will continue to steal from the other side of the grave.

CHAPTER III
The Company

Life in Florida was easy for Lisa, she had settled into her new home with ease, meeting neighbors and making friends. It had been about six months since she and Ryan had ventured into the other world and brought back five hundred thousand dollars in jewels and trinkets. She still had plenty of money but decided to go back. Again, she wasn't sure if it was the money or the adventure of crossing over. Either way, Lisa set out to find a suitable follower.

The upscale bar where Lisa liked to sit was like so many others in Sarasota, Florida, with rich older folks sitting and sipping their drinks and not rich younger folks either, living off their older relatives' money or trying to find a way to get the older relatives' money. Lisa found the spectacle amusing as she sat sipping her martini. That's when Mark caught her eye. She began watching this young man on the other side of the bar after she heard him trying to bet the bartender for drinks.

"I can set this napkin on fire and put it out with my mind." He told the bartender, smiling from ear to ear. The bartender was not impressed and just handed him another beer. He sat quietly and sipped his beer, looking in every direction to find someone to hustle. Lisa motioned the bartender over and bought him another drink. Sure enough, her plan worked, and he came straight over.

"Mark, and you are?" He said as he stuck out his hand to shake.

"Lisa, please, have a seat." Lisa said as womanly as she could.

Mark was a thin man with hair cut just below his ears. It looked like he was in the first clothes he came to as he got dressed. Nothing seemed to match or even go together, but his confidence made it all work. The next several hours were spent talking about themselves. They ended up walking down Main Street and continuing to share what they thought would be important to one another. They finished their evening with Lisa saying, "Goodbye, call me".

The next month was a whirlwind of dating, sex, and spending time together. As time went on, Lisa was becoming increasingly anxious about getting back across. Finally, Lisa sat Mark down one evening and began to share her secret with him.

"We go to Hendersonville Tennessee, and we find a portal. We go through the portal to the other side. There we can take all the jewels, gold and silver we can carry. Then we simply come back through using a different portal, and then, it's easy street for us both." Lisa finished and asked if he would like to be richer than he could ever imagine. Mark just looked at her and smiled, as what she had told him was truly unbelievable.

"Sure!" Mark said, not really believing what she had told him. Mark, though, was always up for an adventure, and this seemed to be that if nothing else.

Lisa had Mark rent a car, and they were off toward Hendersonville. Mark wasn't sure what was happening, but he was willing to go along and see. Lisa had the two empty carry-on bags that were flexible and easy to carry. She went through her small backpack and made sure she had her driver's license, her passport, some cash, a credit card, a knife, and the viewer. They left early in the morning before daylight and drove straight through, only stopping for lunch, gas and snacks. Once in Hendersonville, Mark parked the car at the end of the street, and they were off exploring the town. Lisa was still careful not to run into anyone she knew, so she wouldn't have to answer any questions. As they wandered around town, going into the small shops and looking at the different arts and craft things, clothes and antiques, Lisa kept an eye open for folks she had known in the past. It was while watching for those people that she noticed the car sitting across the street with two men inside it. It reminded her of the day she had left Hendersonville and the man she saw on the porch, who seemed to look right at her and smile.

Lisa and Mark left the shop and headed down the street; they turned at the corner, and Lisa pulled Mark into the first store they came to. It was a pet bakery, and Mark was really confused about being in here, as neither of them had a pet, but he started looking at the items on the shelves. Lisa was pretending to look, but her attention was on the street outside. When she saw the car pull up and park across the street, her heart seemed to stop, and a wave of fear washed over her. Who were they? What did they want? Why were they watching her and Mark? Lisa's mind was racing, so she jumped and screamed when Mark stuck the small dog puppet in her face.

"Oh, I'm sorry honey." Mark said as he grabbed Lisa and hugged her.

I didn't mean to scare you." He said apologetically.

"No, it's not you, it's that car across the street." Lisa said, pointing at the car.

Mark took off out the door before Lisa could stop him. As Mark crossed the street heading for the car, he pulled his phone out and took several pictures of the car and the men inside. The driver sped off, and Mark took a couple of pictures of the car's license plate before the car was gone. Mark stood there in the street watching the car drive away. Now he was wondering what he had gotten himself into. He turned and looked back to see if Lisa was still there. She was standing in the doorway, watching the car drive away too. Mark had a lot of questions when he went back to get Lisa. The problem was that Lisa didn't have any of the answers because she didn't completely know what was going on either. The two of them drove toward the edge of town to a diner where they could sit and wait until dark. In the diner, Mark's questions were relentless.

"Who were those guys? Why were they following us? What the hell is going on? Mark was firing off questions in what felt like an interrogation to Lisa.

"Look, I don't know!" Lisa snapped at Mark.

"Here is what I do know. The person who took me into the other world had a journal, and in the journal, he mentioned the company and that they were chasing him the night we met. That's where the viewer comes from, and I guess they want it back." Lisa said angrily. Mark was about to say something when two men walked up to their table. Another man walked up and scooted in next to Mark, wearing a big smile.

"How y'all doing?" He said as he stared into Lisa's eyes.

Lisa and Mark just sat there looking at the man. Lisa was not impressed with this man. His eyes were too close together, and his chin was long and seemed out of proportion to his face. His shirt was buttoned all the way up with no tie, or bolo tie or anything to give him a reason to button that last button. The thin black jacket he was wearing covered his arms, which Lisa figured were as thin as could be, because his fingers reminded her of a skeleton's fingers. Lisa raised her eyes slowly up to meet his as he began to speak.

"Let me explain everything to y'all so we don't have any real problems." The man said, still smiling and looking straight at Lisa.

"My name is Henry, Henry McDavid, and I grew up in this town. So, when I say this is my town, I mean it." Henry spoke without taking his eyes off Lisa.

"Now I remember seeing you putting a bag in your car the day we found ole, Tim Loudin, dead in his backyard. You looked like you were running from the boogie man, so I figured you had something to do with his demise or at least saw what happened to him." Henry was tapping his thumb on the table as he spoke. The tension in the air was malleable as Lisa wasn't sure what Mark was going to do.

"Now you see, Tim was a prototype of sorts; he was going to stay on the other side and try to figure that side out. Now that he is gone, well, I haven't found anyone else willing to stay there and get me my information." Henry just smiled as he finished speaking.

"So, unless one of you wants to travel over there and stay, then, please, do us all a favor, give me my viewer, get in your car and drive away now, and all is forgotten. If you don't do that, well then, we may have to put you away." Henry finished talking and looked at Mark.

"What is on the other side you want to know about?" Mark asked.

"Other than the gold and silver and stuff?" Mark was not smiling as he spoke.

"Well, that's company business". Henry said, looking back at Lisa. "But I believe there is more there than just money". Henry finished talking and stood up.

Young lady, if you want to talk about joining me and my company, all you have to do is let me know," Henry said, his eyes roaming over Lisa.

"We need that viewer so my guy here will follow you back to your hotel and you can give it to him there." He paused for a moment, smiling at Lisa, then he walked slowly out of the diner.

Lisa and Mark watched the three men walk outside and one of them drove away with Henry. The other man was in a different car waiting for them. Mark just sat and stared at Lisa, not saying a word.

Lisa was figuring out how she would be able to explain this to Mark and have him go through with the crossover.

"The mob." Mark was talking, but that's all Lisa heard.

"We just need to outsmart the mob. Hell, that's easy, I been doing that most of my life". Mark said, laughing under his breath.

Lisa looked at him for a second, then realized she wouldn't have to explain it to Mark. As he has it all figured out already.

"We just need to go early, as soon as it's dark". Mark said, sitting back like he had cracked the code of some big spy ring.

Lisa just nodded as she threw some cash on the table, and they left. As they drove off, they both knew they didn't have a hotel. Mark drove them to a random hotel on the outskirts of town and parked their car in the front so the man who was following them would be able to see it. They went in and waited in the hotel lobby for a bit until the sun was almost gone from the sky. The man waiting in the car had waited long enough and was coming in. Mark and Lisa snuck out the side door and cut through the small patch of trees to the next street over. There, they got an Uber to pick them up and drive them out into the countryside.

After several minutes, they told the driver to stop, and they got out.

"Now what?" Mark asked, looking around in the darkness.

"Now we wait." Lisa said, looking around as she pulled the viewer out and began looking up and down the road.

After just a couple of minutes, Lisa heard the familiar low rustling sound of wind in the trees and then saw a figure being dragged along the road. She handed Mark the viewer and pointed out where to look. As soon as Mark saw the lost soul, he snapped the viewer down from his face and slowly handed it back to Lisa. She could see fear on Mark's face for the first time; it made her smile a little.

"Let's go". She said, grabbing one of the bags while holding the viewer up to her face.

Mark grabbed the other bag, and they headed off following the ragged body. The body suddenly turned off the road and headed into the woods. Lisa and Mark followed close behind it. Then, up ahead, Lisa could see the blue light of the sphere through the viewer.

"There it is just up ahead." Lisa said, quickening her pace to pass the lost soul. Mark followed her closely as they approached the portal. Lisa never stopped walking and was pushing through the portal while pulling Mark through as the body was disappearing into it. As they stood up in the other world, Lisa saw the familiar dead woods but found the smells to be worse than she remembered.

"Follow me." She commanded as she headed off back the way they had just come toward a town's silhouette. The town once again seemed to come at them faster than they were walking toward it. As they walked down the street, Lisa noticed this decaying town was not familiar like Hendersonville, they were in a completely different part of the town on the other side. Have I ever been to this part of town? Lisa thought as she was looking for an open building. As Lisa walked slowly down the street, she realized this was Sarasota, a place she now lived and could die in. Several hundred yards down the street, she found an open building, and they ran inside. Mark had been picking things up as they were walking and sliding them into one of the bags. The floor was littered with jewels and things; Lisa instructed Mark to take the bags and grab as much as he could and stuff it inside the bags until he could barely close the lid. Lisa stood at the door and pretended to watch for anyone or anything to come.

"This would go a lot quicker if you helped me." Mark said as he was stuffing trinkets as fast as he could. Mark was watching Lisa as she stood there in the doorway and just kept working on filling the two bags.

Lisa was looking through the viewer and saw three figures coming down the street. She realized they had been on this side for about seven minutes. She was trying to see who was coming, and as they got closer, she realized they were the souls from this side.

Had they stayed too long? Was there a time limit to a visit?

"We gotta go!" Lisa said as she looked across at Mark.

"Almost got it full." Mark said. Stuffing the last of the jewels in.

Mark zipped the lid shut on the second case, and they took off running toward the edge of town. The souls that were following them didn't seem to be able to move very fast, so they outran them easily. Once in the woods again, Lisa stopped.

"What are you doing?" Mark said as he ran past her.

"We have to wait for a portal." Lisa said, spinning around, looking through the viewer. The souls were coming, and even at their walking pace, they would get there soon enough. Lisa was all but begging for a blue light to show up. She looked back at the souls coming in their direction. She watched through her viewer as the souls simply disappeared. Lisa closed her eyes and looked through the viewer again, but they were gone. Then, just off to their left was a light. Lisa pushed Mark as she headed for the light.

"Go!" she yelled as she pushed Mark through the blue light. Lisa shivered as she passed through the light. When the pressure of the portal was gone, Lisa found herself running down a steep hill and trying to keep her balance. She could see Mark rolling and tumbling down the hill. He still had both cases in his hands.

At the bottom of the hill, they finally stopped and collected themselves. Lisa instinctively hunkered down; Mark followed her lead.

Lisa opened her backpack, put the viewer in its case and took out her phone. She pulled up the location app. and discovered they were in San Juan, Brazil. They were in the rough mountains just east of San Juan. They would have to sneak into San Juan and find a way to get back to Florida. It was early morning, and the sun was just starting to heat the air. The jungle was dense and dark. They continued to push through until late afternoon, when they broke through the jungle and into a field. The couple had walked all day, fighting through the jungle, and were exhausted. As night fell, Lisa decided a flashlight would be a good item to add to her go bag. After an hour or more of walking in the field, they came to a small road with two tire paths, which led them to the edge of San Juan.

"Finally," Mark said, breaking the silence from before. Lisa was not in a talking mood as she was worried about getting back to Florida with two bags of unexplained jewels. As they walked into San Juan, they were looking for anything or anyone that would be friendly to Americans. After wandering through the town for what seemed like an hour. They found a resort hotel for cruise ships and tourists, and they went in. Lisa had Mark rent the room on his credit card. It was just before midnight, and Lisa wanted to get Mark into the room before they came for him. After settling in, they started working on a plan to get back to Florida. Mark thought they could just rent a car and drive to the coast, then charter a boat home. Lisa knew Mark wouldn't have to worry about it, as he was headed back to the other side.

Lisa went down to the desk and talked with a manager about getting a private jet back to Florida. The manager was very helpful and agreed to schedule her private jet for the next day in the afternoon. Knowing that Mark would be gone by the time she left. She told the manager her partner would be staying for a few more days and would book his own flight from the airport.

Lisa went back to the room exhausted. She was moving slowly, killing time and waiting till Mark was gone. In the room, Lisa noticed a smell she didn't like, so she opened both balcony doors to let fresh air flow into the room. She was listening to Mark, who was going on about what they were going to do once they were back in the States, and how they could process the jewels quickly.

"I know a guy who'll take it all and give us straight cash," Mark said from the other room.

"A fence, if you will. I mean, this stuff isn't stolen, but it isn't legit either." Mark was fumbling through the jewels as he talked. Lisa was in the bathroom when she heard the low rustle of wind in the trees. She stepped out and grabbed the viewer to watch. Mark's body fell back on the couch as his soul was taken, and his empty, lifeless body went limp. Lisa watched his soul rise up, and it seemed to float there for a moment, then Mark's soul seemed to drift slowly over to the open balcony door and out, where it just slowly drifted out of sight. Lisa casually walked over, lifted Mark's legs onto the couch and put a blanket over him. She decided to sleep for a few hours and laid down across the bed. The next morning, she took out her journal. The company was onto her and wanted the viewer back. Henry had mentioned there was more on the other side than just money, but what? Lisa thought as she was writing in the journal. She realized that Mark had a point about getting the jewels to a fence, selling them all at once. Lisa closed the journal and began gathering all her stuff. Later that day, she took her bags and headed for the lobby. She put the do not disturb sign on the door and gave the housekeeper a fifty-dollar bill to stay away from their room. Lisa got a car to drive her to the airport. She was watching the people as they drove through the small streets of San Juan. They were moving in their own directions, living their lives day to day with no idea of what was in store for them when they passed over to the other side.

As Lisa boarded the jet, she had an idea for future trips. She would hire a jet the next time to be on standby and come to wherever she was to bring her home. As the jet lifted off, she was reading what she had written in her journal, all the details she had from this trip, including the run-in with the company. She would need a better plan next time to avoid those guys. She also wrote how, after so long on the other side, the souls seemed to be coming after them. Then they just disappeared. Lisa closed her journal and laid her head back to sleep and dreamed about her trips through the grave.

CHAPTER IV

It's All in the Details

Lisa found herself sitting on the side of the bed at two in the morning. Hands trembling as she pulled herself back into reality, assuring herself that she was fine. Lisa had started having dreams about being trapped on the other side after she returned from the last trip. In her dreams, she was stuck in one of the open buildings on the other side. The lost souls were clamoring to get to her, and just as they did, she would wake up. If this was the result of being on the other side, she wasn't sure she would ever go back in. She laid back down in bed and tried to relax back into sleep.

The next morning, Lisa decided to look at her notes from the last crossover and see if she could put anything together to help her feel better about going back over. She took her journal from its hiding place, taped inside a kitchen cabinet behind a drawer. As she opened it, she started remembering how the souls were coming to apparently get her and Mark. Why did they do this? More than that, where did they go? She thought, thumbing through the pages. Had they taken too many jewels? Did they make too much noise? Was it the building they chose? Lisa sat and thought hard about that incident. She remembered Mark saying if you helped me, this would go faster. That must be it; they were on the other side too long. The souls had time to realize they were there and taking their riches. How long was she in there, five minutes, twenty-five minutes? She never thought about timing it. She thought back to when she went over with Tim for the first time. He was in such a hurry. This must be why, somehow, Tim knew there was a timeframe for being over there, but how? The company, she thought. The company must know all this stuff, and they go over all the time and are taking lots of people over to take the jewels, then letting those people die. Lisa closed the journal and started working through the list of problems and her solutions to them. What else was there other than riches? Henry's words kept ringing inside her head. I need to get away from here, where I can think through all of this. Lisa threw a bag together, got in her car and headed south.

Later that evening, Lisa was walking down Duvall Street in Key West, Florida, wondering if she needed to go back over to the other side again. She knew she had to because the money she had collected from selling the jewelry wouldn't be enough to keep her in her current living style and status forever. Maybe she needed the excitement of crossing over, or both. She just had to figure out how to do it and not get caught by the company in Hendersonville. She needed to find a system that worked so she could make the crossing as often as she needed. Lisa stopped in a local bar and sat quietly sipping on a bourbon and watching people. She began to overhear conversations between the people seated next to her. One table to her right had two obvious businessmen seated at it; they were discussing the plan to take over a smaller rival company. She heard one of the men say this would give us all the buying power if we could get the deal closed. The table behind her had a man and a woman seated at it; they were discussing their siblings and how, if they could get the power of attorney, they would have all the power over the family and its money and business. That's it, she thought, power was the other commodity on the other side. Her mind began to race with ideas. What if you could control the other side? Could you control deaths on this side? Decide who dies and who lives. Having control over the other side could give one person control of both worlds. Lisa sat on her balcony over Duvall Street the entire next day, trying to figure out what all these new revelations meant. She realized she had no idea because she didn't know what else was truly on the other side. She decided to go home and try to find out all she could about the company and what they knew about the other side.

Once back in Sarasota, she started searching on the internet, but after several days of trying to find anything, she realized she couldn't find anything at all. The company was either really good at hiding their electronic footprint or they didn't have one.

Could they really do this without touching the internet? She thought as she sat at her desk. Lisa didn't think they could, but she didn't have the skill set to find them on her own. What if I build my own company, sharing the wealth and making a few other special people rich. That's it, she needed help, and she believed she knew where to find it.

In Hendersonville, a few years ago, she had briefly dated a guy who was a computer whiz. Rick Walker was his name, and he had left Hendersonville for a high-paying job in California. Hence, the end of their short relationship. I need to find Rick; she thought as she looked at the clock and noticed it was three thirty-seven in the morning. Lisa dragged herself into bed and collapsed into a deep sleep as she felt she had found a big piece of her puzzle.

The next day, Lisa began trying to reconnect with Rick. She tried Facebook, TikTok, X, all the platforms she could think of, but could not find him. She called his sister in Hendersonville, but all she knew was that he had gone to California, and her family hadn't heard from him in a couple of years. They asked Lisa to find him and bring him home if she could. Lisa decided she would go to Silicon Valley and find Rick.

Lisa landed in San Francisco and headed for Stanford University as she figured that would be a good place to start. The Uber driver dropped her off at the front office and drove away. Standing there looking all around, Lisa realized she had no idea of how to find Rick. She didn't even know what company he was working for, or if he was still here at all. She also realized she shouldn't have come to the university and was now wondering why she did. Lisa had a couple of hours to kill before she could check in to her hotel, so she walked over to a bench and sat down. Realizing she had come here without an idea, a lead, or even a plan, she felt like giving up. Lisa sat there desperately trying to remember anything Rick had told her about where he was going or what he was doing. She remembered how Rick was always talking about Bill Gates and Microsoft and what a great company it was.

"Finally, a place to start," Lisa mumbled under her breath as she stood up and started walking. After just a few steps, she stopped and looked all around her. She realized she had no idea where she was going. She grabbed her phone and ordered an Uber.

The Uber dropped her off in front of the Microsoft building. Lisa straightened her clothes and tried to look professional as she rolled her suitcase through the front door. There was a large desk with two women behind it and three security guards standing around the large room. Several people were sitting on the big, fluffy couches with small round tables in front of them. All were on a computer or their phone. Lisa walked up to the front desk and cleared her throat.

"I'm looking for Rick Walker." Lisa said, looking at the security guard behind the counter.

"I'm sorry, ma'am, but I don't know a Rick Walker, and even if I did, we can't give out any information about our employees." The young lady behind the counter smiled as she finished talking.

Lisa didn't know what to do next, so she walked over to the door and stood there thinking for a moment. She figured she would go to the hotel and get checked in. Then, go get a bite of dinner and see if she could come up with a plan for the next day.

Once back at the hotel, Lisa fell across her bed and began thinking about how she could find a computer tech guy, even if she couldn't find Rick. She decided that if she couldn't find Rick or come up with a good lead, she would head back to Florida and find another way. She grabbed her purse and headed for the door, realizing she was starving. She went to the front desk and asked the valet where he would go eat if he could go.

"I'm a mom-and-pop kind of guy, so I would go to the Lazy Lamb. All the locals go there." The valet said, smiling.

"Got it." Lisa said as she climbed inside the cab.

At the Lazy Lamb, Lisa was taken aback by how old and dated everything was. She thought this place must've been here forever. She looked at the hostess and pointed to the bar. She slowly walked over to an empty seat. She pulled up her stool and grabbed the menu. She ordered a couple of appetizers and a stiff drink. She sat there eating her appetizer and trying to order another stiff drink, then she heard a familiar voice say.

"Lisa, Lisa Riley, is that you?" She turned to see Rick standing beside her. She couldn't believe her luck; she was so struck by Rick standing there next to her that she froze for a moment.

"Uh, hi." That was all she could muster up.

"What are you doing here?" Rick asked, moving in closer to get out of the walkway.

"Look, looking for you." Lisa said, still reeling from the shock of running into Rick like this.

"I have something to talk to you about." Lisa said as she stood up from the bar and hugged Rick. Lisa walked with Rick back to his table. Rick was sitting with some colleagues having drinks. He introduced her to everyone, and Lisa was pleasant, but she really couldn't have cared less. She was remembering Rick's body and how good he had been in bed. She was zoned out and breathing in Rick's manly scent when she noticed one of the guys at the table waving. Lisa smiled and waved back. Rick took her by the arm and led her to a different table.

"Wow, it is so good to see you." Rick said, smiling and staring at Lisa. The restaurant was loud, and Lisa didn't want to shout.

"Is there someplace quieter we can go?" she asked Rick.

"Sure." Rick said, looking a bit concerned at Lisa's request. Rick paid for their drinks, and they walked outside. There was an instant, relieving wave of quiet that washed over both of them. They turned and started walking quietly down the street, under the streetlights. Lisa looked at Rick and smiled.

"It's good to see you, Rick." Lisa said, smiling. Lisa had rehearsed this spiel several times on her way to find Rick, but now that he was standing right in front of her, she didn't even know where to start.

"So, what have you been up to Rick?" Lisa asked as they slowly walked.

"I have been working here in the valley. I've been at a couple of places, but I'm just another geeky computer guy out here." Rick said, sounding a little sad.

"What about you Lisa?" Rick asked.

"Oh, you know the usual, following lost souls through portals to other dimensions." Lisa said, chuckling. There was a pause as Rick wasn't sure what she meant by that. Lisa realized he had stopped walking and was just staring at her.

"I need your help, Rick." she said as they sat down on a bench under a large tree.

"Sure, if I can help, I will." Rick said with a serious look on his face.

Lisa began to tell Rick about her idea of putting together a team to build wealth. I have found a way to gather up old jewelry and sell it in very large quantities. She hesitated to tell him about the other side, though she knew he would need to know sooner or later. This team will travel to unique places and gather wealth. I need you because you know computers and the internet. After she told him this watered-down version, she smiled and stood up. Rick was just staring up at her, not sure of what he had just heard or if he believed any of it.

"I'm going to breakfast tomorrow morning at nine in my hotel restaurant. I hope to see you there, but if not, I'll head back. Just know it was good to see you either way." Lisa was looking very serious. She finished talking, Rick stood up and hugged her, and she walked away.

Rick walked back to the bar to have another round with his friends, but he wasn't the same now. Lisa had given him just enough information to make him wonder about what she was talking about. Rick didn't sleep much that night as his mind was going on and on about the things she had said. Portals, other dimensions, gathering up jewelry. What did it all mean, he thought as he sat in bed staring at his phone.

The next morning, as Lisa was walking into the little breakfast nook at the hotel, she stopped and looked all around but didn't see Rick anywhere. She felt disappointed as she poured a cup of coffee. She sat down at a small table, but hadn't noticed Rick sitting out in the lobby watching her. Rick was waiting to see if anyone else was with Lisa or if she was making eye contact with anyone. He watched her for four or five minutes. When he was satisfied, she was alone, he stood and started walking over to Lisa. Lisa caught him standing up and smiled as he walked over.

"Were you spying on me?" She asked, smiling. Rick slowly pulled out his chair and sat down.

"I guess I was. I just wanted to make sure you were alone. Computer analysts like me are being watched, questioned, arrested, and sometimes they just disappear." Rick said, staring right into Lisa's eyes.

"Well, I'm not looking to do anything but make you rich." Lisa said smiling.

The two just sat there looking at each other for a moment, then Lisa began telling Rick about her enterprise.

"What if I told you I could make you richer than you could ever imagine?" Lisa said, half smiling.

"Go on." Rick said, sitting up in his seat.

Lisa began telling Rick about the viewer, lost souls and the portals to another dimension. About the other side and how they could make more money than anyone has ever had. Rick just sat and stared at her, and she wasn't sure what he was thinking, so she just kept talking. After several minutes, Rick raised his hand to stop Lisa from talking. Realizing she had barely taken a breath, let alone paused, Lisa stopped talking and sat back in her chair. Rick sat there quietly without saying anything for a moment, then he just smiled and nodded his head.

"Where do I sign up?" Rick said with a big smile.

"My life and work are both so boring right now that what you're talking about, although it makes no sense whatsoever, it's an adventure. I'm so ready for some adventure." Rick finished talking, and they both seemed to relax.

Rick stood up and grabbed Lisa's bag.

"Let's go back to my place and get this started." He said as he turned for the door. Lisa took off and caught up to him, and they walked a couple of blocks to Rick's car.

Back at Rick's house, they went inside. Lisa was amazed at all the computer stuff that was sitting around. She recognized some of it for what it was, but most of it was just computer stuff.

"What do we do first?' Rick asked as he was turning on his equipment.

Lisa looked around the room one more time and began fumbling through her purse for her notes. She handed the small notepad to Rick, who opened it and began reading about the company. After several minutes, he turned on three of his computer monitors and began typing.

Henry McDavid, Hendersonville, Tennessee, and Lisa watched as Rick typed the name and location into a search engine.

"What pictures?" He asked, never looking up from his computer's screens. Lisa grabbed her purse and started fumbling around in it until she produced Mark's phone.

"They're on here." Lisa said, holding the phone up. Rick held out his hand, and she put the phone in it. Rick took the phone and plugged it into a machine that searched for the password. In only a few seconds, the machine beeped, and Rick typed in the password, and the phone opened. Rick went straight to the pictures and found the ones of the guys in the car and the license plate.

He somehow waved the phone at his computer, and the pictures just went into his computer. Rick turned the phone back off and handed it to Lisa.

"Destroy this," Rick said, not looking up from his screens. Lisa was watching and smiling as Rick continued with his searches. After a few seconds, Rick sat back and said this should only take a minute. Lisa was staring at Rick and smiling. After a few minutes of silence, Rick sat up and began to read the screen.

"The man in the car was Tony Ridel, and the car was registered to him. Henry McDavid is a convicted felon living in Hendersonville with a pretty big list of crimes, including assault with a deadly weapon. He owns a small business called Crossover that handles imports for the local stores in the Hendersonville area." As Rick was talking, he started typing again and started a search for the company's financial records, tax forms and so on.

After several minutes, he started printing things, soon they had all the public financial records of Henry's company. Henry's company was taking in much more money than their imports could ever generate. They were depositing the money from their company and the extra funds into a bank there in Hendersonville. From there, they were investing in large and small businesses, they owned several restaurants and even one casino in Las Vegas. Lisa was impressed by Rick's quick work; however, this information didn't help her get past the company so she could grab her own jewels. Lisa began thinking about a strategy to get past Henry and his goons. She walked over to the table and began writing her thoughts down about the process. After several minutes, Rick came over and sat down across from her. He sat there quietly watching Lisa write, scribble and erase frantically.

"What!" Lisa finally snapped as she stopped writing and sat back in her chair. Rick reached across the table and pulled Lisa's pad toward him. He read the couple of sentences that were legible and slid it back across the table.

"So, let's see. You are only interested in finding a way to go around Henry and his company, correct?" Rick said, looking straight at Lisa. Lisa just nodded, not looking up from her pad. Rick went on to explain how, from just the little bit of searching he had done, he could tell that Henry's company was not very organized. They were allowing things to be on the internet that shouldn't be on the internet. Rick figured their day-to-day operations would be just as disorganized. So, it would be fairly easy to get around Henry and his company. They were also using old methods to hide the money. Rick had better ideas that would allow them to surpass Henry's company and crush them.

Lisa looked at him and smiled, sending Rick the signal he needed to get started on his methods of money handling.

The next day, Rick began searching for jewelers, pawn shops and collectors to sell the stuff Lisa would bring back. He would set up accounts to move the money into. He started explaining how unregulated personal banking accounts are if they stay under a certain amount, so they would need several of them. Lisa stopped him and laid out her part of the plan.

"I have several accounts with my money in them and a big pile of jewels left to get rid of at my house in Florida. I will fly there and bring jewels here so we can begin our enterprise. Lisa said as she pulled her phone out to book the flight. Lisa checked out of her hotel and left the next day for Sarasota. She wasted no time in renting a car and loading up the jewels to start the drive back out to California. On the way there, she could really see how she and Rick could put this thing together and crush the company, while at the same time making themselves rich.

A couple of days later, Lisa pulled into Rick's driveway and carried the bag of jewels in. It was less than one carry-on bag full now, though it seemed like more than enough to impress Rick.

"You start selling this, and I'll go back over and get some more." Lisa said as she stacked the suitcase on one of the kitchen chairs. Rick looked at Lisa with a scared look on his face. Lisa shook her head and took Rick's hand.

"You're not going over there; I need you here to continue to build this company." Lisa was looking deep into Rick's eyes as she spoke. Rick smiled and nodded in agreement.

"First thing I need is a person to go with me, a follower if you will." Lisa said, grabbing her purse to head out. She noticed that Rick was looking a bit puzzled at this statement, so she decided to tell him everything.

"Look, there are crossers, and there are followers. I am a crosser, and as long as I don't grab, take or even touch the jewels on the other side, I am safe. The follower is the one who grabs the stuff over there. They fill the bags and carry them back across. Somewhere between forty-eight and seventy-two hours after we get back on this side here, they send one of their lost souls over to take the soul of the follower." Lisa finished talking and just stared at Rick. She went on to explain how she would get a guy to go with her to the other side and gather and carry all the stuff back. His soul would be taken back to the other side the next day. Rick sat with his hand over his mouth as he listened to Lisa.

"So, people will die doing this?" he asked.

"I prefer to think of it as they are taken to the other side to live forever. I'm really doing them a favor." Lisa said with a small smile.

"Well, in that case, okay then." Rick said, shaking his head.

Lisa went out that night and found a young man named John, and they started seeing one another. Lisa was in a hurry so, after only about a week, she told him about the trip to Hendersonville and that she could make him rich beyond his biggest dreams. It took a couple more days before Lisa felt John was ready to follow her to Hendersonville and the other side. As she explained her plan to get to Hendersonville, she realized John's arms seemed bigger than they should be, and his shoulders were massive too. His high and tight haircut didn't do him justice though. Lisa thought he should let it grow out a bit. Too bad there wouldn't be time for that, she thought as she was booking their flights. John was the kind of person though, that once he made his mind up to do something, he was all in. Ex-military and gung-ho for anything that sounded dangerous.

They flew into Nashville this time and rented a car, then drove to Gallatin, Tennessee just outside of Hendersonville. There they bought two carry-on-sized bags. John was ready to take on the world for Lisa. Lisa just needed him to follow her through this crossover. The night of the same day they had arrived, they drove out to the same country road Lisa had been on several times now. Lisa had planned for this trip and had brought a watch to wear so she could mark the time spent over there. They hid John's rental car behind a church and set off to walk the last mile or so. When they were in the spot, Lisa pulled John off the main road into the scrub brush, and they waited. Lisa was looking through the viewer and saw two blue lights out in the distance, but they were much too far out to get to. They ventured back up on the road and started slowly walking down the road. Suddenly, there it was, the low rustle of the wind in the trees. She was trying to look in every direction through the viewer so she wouldn't miss anything. When she saw the twisted soul, it was right next to her, startling her. John grabbed the viewer out of her hand and looked through it.

"What the hell is...?" He was trying to speak but could only mutter a few words.

"Run!" Lisa yelled as she grabbed the viewer and took off behind this poor soul. They followed it deep into the woods until Lisa saw the blue sphere, and they ran past the lost soul. Lisa crouched down to run through the portal, and she glanced at her watch, eleven-thirty-seven. She pushed on through the portal, and John followed. On the other side, John was taken aback by what he saw and smelled. Lisa grabbed his shirt and pulled him in the direction they had come. After a short walk, the town again seemed to be coming at Lisa. They headed down the street until Lisa saw an open building and ran inside.

"We don't have much time." Lisa said as she pushed John toward the open front room of the building.

"I'll watch the door. You grab jewels and stuff as much as you possibly can into those two bags." Lisa was pointing at the floor as she finished and turned her attention to the dark street outside. She looked down at her watch. Eleven-thirty-seven had time had stopped, she thought as she stood there.

John was working as fast as he could, grabbing handfuls of jewels and stuffing them into the carry-on bags. After a few minutes, he zipped the last one shut and ran back towards Lisa.

Let's go!" Lisa said, running back out onto the street. John was full of adrenaline and was running a good twenty feet in front of Lisa when they reached the woods.

"Wait!" Lisa said in a loud whisper. "We have to wait for the next portal to open."

Lisa took the viewer out and began scanning the woods. As they stood there, Lisa began to make out a group of souls through the viewer, moving slowly toward her and John. She noticed John was grabbing jewels from the ground and stuffing them into his pockets. As the souls got closer, she was thinking about running deeper into the woods. The two of them started walking into the woods. Lisa was turning her head back and forth, looking back at the souls as they walked slowly. Lisa was looking through the viewer for the next portal they could get to. Suddenly, there it was, only twenty feet from them. Lisa pushed John in the direction, and they made their way to the portal. With a little force, they both passed through the portal and found themselves on a busy street in the middle of the day.

"Hide!" That was all Lisa could think of saying as she pushed John into an alley. They crouched down between a dumpster and a pile of trash. Lisa took out her phone and pulled up her location. "Cumilla, Bangladesh!" Lisa snorted.

"Where is Bangladesh?" Lisa asked the universe.

"South Aisa." John said. "Hah, we're in Asia." John said excitedly, Lisa just stared at him. Lisa put on her backpack, and each one took a carry-on bag, and they made themselves look presentable. Lisa did a double check to make sure there were no chains or anything sticking out of the bags as they walked out of the alley and started down the street.

Lisa felt for her backpack to make sure she still had it with her; it had her passport, money, credit card, and ID, so she could get back home and of course, the viewer. For now, they needed to find a room, so they walked back onto the street and headed for the nearest hotel. Lisa had John get them a room. Once inside, John was like a little kid, so excited he opened the cases and was trying to guess how much money each piece of jewels would bring. Lisa closed the cases and zipped them up.

"This is not the time to celebrate." She said, closing the bag.

"We are in a foreign land with two suitcases full of maybe hundreds of thousands of dollars. Once we're home, then we can get excited." Lisa finished her sentence as she was sitting down in the chair. She knew she had to figure out a way to get home. She pulled out her phone and searched for the nearest airport and private jet. She found a pilot who would take her to Taiwan, from there she could get a flight back to the United States. She booked the trip to Taiwan for late the next day. Time for a shower and some sleep.

The next day, Lisa awoke late in the morning to the sound of wind rustling through the trees. She knew very well what it was and just laid there with her eyes closed. John never made it out of his bed before the soul taker came for his soul. Lisa got up and started getting ready for the trip to Taiwan. She meticulously went through her bag to make sure she didn't leave any clues of her being tied to the dead body she was going to be leaving in this room. As she was putting the viewer back in her backpack, she held it up to look through it for no real reason other than she had it in her hand. Lisa was startled and jumped up from her chair. Through the viewer, she could see John's soul floating around the room. Why was it still here? Lisa thought as she put the viewer in her backpack and started gathering up her stuff. Lisa just wanted out of this room and was almost in a panic to get there. She grabbed everything and rushed out the door. She was almost running down the hallway when she got ahold of herself and slowed down to a walk.

As Lisa walked out onto the busy street, in the early afternoon with her two bags stuffed full of jewels, she felt nervous but continued till she found a small restaurant. There she grabbed a bite to eat, some coffee and found someone who could speak a little English. It took her a few minutes, but she finally got the person, a young man, to help her get a cab. She headed out toward the airport. The ride to the airport was about thirty minutes, and she got to see some of the town she was in. There seemed to be so many people, all moving in different directions. It again made her think of the lost souls on the other side. All of them move in different directions, with no visible purpose or meaning. She found herself comparing the two sides of the portal. Which one was real? Which one was important? How could she control anything in either of them? The car suddenly jerked to the left as they turned sharply into the airport lane, jerking Lisa back into reality and where she was.

Once in the airport, Lisa checked in and found a seat to wait in. The day wore on, and Lisa's thoughts were all over the place. She was thinking about the souls on the other side and what they were doing there. She was comparing them with the people on this side and what we are doing here. Were we the same, just in different places? She also found herself thinking about Rick. She was happy he was back in her life. He made her feel safe; she smiled thinking about him. The small jet pulled in, and she walked out onto the tarmac and loaded her stuff. She climbed into the cabin and sat back in the comfy seat. Shortly, she took off for Taiwan. The airport in Taiwan was much bigger, and Lisa had no idea where to go or how to get a flight from here to home. The copilot of the plane had gotten off and was walking inside, so Lisa followed her. At the desk, the young man spoke English, so Lisa was able to ask about a flight to California. The copilot interrupted her to let her know they were flying back to California from here with one stop in Honolulu for fuel, and she could ride with them, for a fee, of course. Lisa was relieved and quickly accepted the copilot's invitation. Once back in California, she rented a car and was on her way home to Rick's house. She pulled into his driveway as the sun was going down and just sat there for a minute. Rick came out of the house and opened her door. She looked up at him and smiled.

"It's all in the trunk." She said, pointing the fob at the trunk as she pushed the button. They carried everything inside, and Lisa let out a long sigh. Rick opened the cases up, and they were stuffed full of all sorts of jewels, precious metal and stones. Rick just looked at Lisa, smiled and nodded. Lisa decided to keep the rental car, she wanted nothing but a shower and some rest.

Lisa spent the next day resting at the house, sitting on the covered patio, floating in the pool, or simply sitting on the couch and staring. Meanwhile, Rick had been out selling the jewels. He had the money for most of the jewels; it just needed to be put into their accounts. The best way to do that was to make small, insignificant deposits in lots of banks, over a period of time. He had opened several accounts with several banks, and while Lisa was resting, he had been out making these deposits. Once the money was all in there, he would be able to transfer it to a main account with their business name on it and from there, they could do whatever they liked with the money. Rick took Lisa out for a nice dinner, and they seemed to be reconnecting and maybe rekindling their old relationship.

The next morning, Rick showed all the nuts and bolts of this process to Lisa, explained that both of their names were on the accounts, and that meant either of them could deposit, move and withdraw money. Later that day, when Lisa felt better, she inquired about the company and whether Rick had discovered any information. Rick looked at her and smiled.

"I have a friend in Hendersonville who gave me the inside story." Rick said with a cocky grin.

Rick started, "The company was started back in twenty-twenty by this guy named Henry McDavid. It seems there was a scientist named Nathan Ashton who discovered a new lens to see dark light through. According to what I read, darkness is not just the absence of light, it has many different light waves. This new lens is the reason you can see the souls and portals. As this scientist was getting his copyrights and things in order to go public, apparently, Henry McDavid found out about it, took the lens and figured out how to cross over to the other side without dying. The scientist has disappeared without a trace and is either dead or being held by the company. Now, Henry McDavid is the guy in charge, and this is how it works. They recruit people to go with what they call a guide and grab as much jewelry and stuff as they can and carry it back, on the promise of half the money. Then the recruit gets killed or taken back over or whatever. Leaving the stuff with the guide who brings it back, and they launder it the same way we are laundering ours. They have a large group of guides, recruiters, accountants, and lawyers. The accountants and lawyers are not in the main group; they just protect the company from things and handle the money. It seems to be a pretty lawless group, though with Henry McDavid calling all the shots." When Rick finished, Lisa just sat and stared at him for several seconds.

"Who is your friend from Hendersonville?" Lisa asked, staring out the window.

"Just a guy we went to school with." Rick said.

Lisa knew there was only one way Rick's friend could know all of this; he had to be a part of it. Lisa didn't know what Rick had told him about what they were doing, but she knew the company was coming.

"We have to get out of here, now!" Lisa said as she jumped up and started shoving things into a bag.

"Why, what are you doing?" Rick asked, seemingly very confused.

"There is only one way your friend would know all this information. He must be with the company!" Lisa shouted.

"What did you tell him about us?" Lisa demanded.

"Nothing, I told him I had heard about this years ago and was wondering if that's it, I swear." Rick said, following Lisa around.

Lisa's mind was racing as she was going from room to room, grabbing what she thought they would need. The money, the rest of the jewels, the banking stuff, computers, phones, her journal. Rick was just standing there looking at her.

"We are fine." Rick said they have no idea where we are or what we are doing.

Lisa stopped and glared at Rick for several seconds.

"How long did it take you find Henry McDavid's name and address?" Lisa asked. Rick just stood there looking at her, he was realizing they would be able to trace him from his conversation and were probably on their way now.

"Oh shit, I'm sorry!" Rick shouted.

"Don't be sorry, just grab the important stuff and put it in my car." Lisa said as she was grabbing everything she could.

They worked for several chaotic minutes, and finally, they had everything loaded up and were ready to go.

"We will take separate cars and go in separate directions. Meet me in Paris, Texas in seven days. Lisa said as she backed the car out of the driveway.

Rick turned and went back into the house to look around one last time. Lisa saw him through the rearview mirror, so she pulled over to make sure he got away. Rick walked back out onto the small porch; Lisa heard a distant shot and watched Rick fall dead. Lisa put her car in drive and slowly pulled out, and drove off. She never saw the person shooting or cared to see if they were coming to the house.

She headed toward her house in Florida, but then realized they may have gotten that little detail from Rick as well. So, she decided to stop in Vegas and put a plan together.

CHAPTER V

The Lens

Lisa was driving toward Vegas, and she had this one thought in her head, it was the lens. How was it created? Why was it created? She began to wonder about it since it appeared central to everything. Was it created to be able to cross over or was it created, and then the portals were found. Lisa felt like this might be a good place to start trying to understand everything she knew. She made it as far as Bakersfield, and with all of this on her mind, she decided to stop for the night. In Bakersfield, she grabbed a hotel room and settled in. She went through Rick's things and found an entire folder entitled The Lens. Lisa ordered a pizza, a bottle of wine and opened the file. Rick had found all kinds of stuff and had printed it all. Thank you, Rick, Lisa thought as she looked up. Lisa started reading the information. There were two parts to it the scientific stuff, talking about how the lenses were made, and a kind of journal written by Nathan himself.

In twenty eighteen, a young scientist, Nathan Ashton, just out of Harvard, thinks there is something to contact lenses that people use to enhance colors and sight for athletes, and color-blind people. He starts experimenting with different gases like Argon, Nitrogen, Krypton, and Sulphur and different colored lenses. The process was long and tedious. Nathan would choose the color of the lens and put two of them together, then fill the space between the lenses with different gases and mixtures of gases. He stumbles upon the new discovery by accident when his tank of mixed Argon, Krypton and Sulphur gas starts leaking. As he is trying to get the leak stopped, he looked through the open gas and through several colored lenses he has on the workbench. Through one of the green lenses, he saw a dim wavey blue light in the darkness at the back of his workbench. Nathan was surprised, happy and terrified at the same time because he had no idea what he had just discovered. This started his work toward inventing his dark light lens. He tried several different mixtures of the gases. A ratio mix of Argon, Krypton, and Sulphur with a green lens was the one that produced the blue light. Unlike night vision goggles, these lenses need no external light to make them work, they could see the blue light waves already present in the darkness. That blue light was enough to see silhouettes and other features in the darkest of conditions. So, the creation of his dark light lens allowed him to not only see the portals but also see ghosts, or other beings, or whatever the hell they were. Lisa found an entry in Nathan's journal where Nathan realized he had stumbled onto something that could change the world and the belief system of mankind. Nathan wrote, *suppose one of those ghost-hunting shows actually discovered a spirit. Just suppose they found proof of an afterlife. The mere knowledge changes our understanding of physics and the nature of consciousness.*

What Nathan has discovered is that even in the dark, there is plenty of light, it's just that the human eye can't detect it. His lens allows us to not only see the light waves but to capture photos in the darkest of nights. This technology could be used by the military to see at night for all sorts of things.

Nathan contacted his friend Henry McDavid and showed him how to use the lens. Not knowing how he should proceed, he hoped that Henry would help him. Henry took the lens and began looking into the night. He started at an old church, just outside of Hendersonville. Thinking a cemetery would be a good place to look for things at night. That is where he saw the first human spirit being dragged across the small cemetery. He can't believe what he is seeing. He tests what he is seeing by turning on a flashlight, the aberration disappears. It's only when the night is so dark that the human eye can't see anything that the lens picks up the ghost. Henry goes to several haunted places to find actual ghosts, and he finds almost nothing. Then, one night, Henry was driving back into Hendersonville and was looking through the lens as he drove. That's when he saw another ragged body being dragged along the road and into the woods. When Henry told Nathan what he had seen, they decided they needed to know for sure what they were looking at. Was it a real ghost, spirit or soul? Henry contacted a friend who was a nurse in a hospice facility. He told her he was helping a scientist who was working on the moment of death changes to the human body. After a small bribe, she let the two men set up their lens in the room of a man who was truly at the end of life. The two of them sat quietly in the dark with the man. They each had a lens, and Nathan had set up a camera and was recording. At seven minutes after two in the morning, the man let out a loud exhale. Nathan watched through the lens as the man's soul rose slowly up and started drifting off like a puff of smoke set adrift on the wind. The man's soul drifted slowly toward the outer wall of the room. According to Nathan's notes, he and Henry watched this soul drift around the room until the door was opened by the nurse. The soul seemed to be sucked out as it left the room and went into the lighted hallway, where in the light it disappeared. The soul can't leave or even move with its own power. It's adrift on the air currents that explain why spirits stay in a building where they died. They literally can't get out until the air flow pushes or sucks them out. Reading this sent chills up Lisa's back, but she kept on reading. Lisa paused and wondered if John was still drifting around in the hotel in Bangladesh. Knowing now that it was human souls they were seeing, they captured these ghosts and what turned out to be the portals on film, trying to build enough proof to convince the scientific world of the existence of an afterlife, although they don't know what it is or how it works. Having proof of an afterlife, Nathan and Henry are ready to go public, looking for more funding to study this new discovery and the right people to explore it. Though Nathan's intentions are good, he is trying to figure out what this new dimension is. Henry wondered if this new technology could be used for his own gain; he just needed to know more about those portals and where those souls go when they enter them. Henry convinces Nathan to wait until he has a chance to investigate the portals before he goes public. With Nathan temporarily stopped, Henry talks one of his prison buddies into going with him through one of the portals.

Lisa was jolted back into reality by the loud bang on the hotel room door. It was her pizza and wine. She tipped the young man and closed and locked the door. She was looking over her notes as she ate a piece of pizza. This Nathan guy really likes to write everything down, she thought as she went for a second slice of pizza. After she finished eating and walked around the room stretching a bit, she sat back down to read the rest of what Nathan had written in his journal.

Henry and his friend took the lens and went back to the place where Henry had seen the ragged soul being dragged. It looks like it took a couple of nights for them to figure out how to get to a portal by following the ragged soul and running through the portal before the soul got to it. On the other side, Henry must've had his friend gather up the jewels, or his friend may have gathered as much as he could carry by himself. Either way, there is no mention of the friend past that night, which means they probably came and took him the next day. Henry must've been with the man when they came and took him, and he figured out that as long as he didn't take the jewels, he would be fine.

When Henry came back to Nathan, he had a plan. Poor Nathan didn't know that at the time. He convinced Nathan that if this were to get out, it would destroy the world as we know it. Henry presented Nathan with this scenario.

If we make this public, the world falls into complete chaos as each religious group feels their holy book and teachings are correct. As it always has been, they are willing to go to war to prove their beliefs in peace and harmony are right. Everything humans said they believed in now would be challenged. Humans would be challenged as the written words of all religions say to live in peace and love one another in some version. Every human would now be challenged with the fact that there is an afterlife, therefore we need to live by the written words. This, however, would prove to be impossible for most, as each religion tries to impose its beliefs about getting to heaven or hell on the masses.

Who is right? Does an afterlife necessarily tie to a religious belief? Or is it simply another level of consciousness that we now can see but don't understand, and can't contact yet.

As the world falls into a chaotic war zone where no one can be trusted, and no one is safe. Towns and cities are destroyed. The country's borders are disappearing. The general rules of humanity are being tossed out, and new ones are being forced on the weak. Cultures are changing as they try to adapt to new ideas and principles.

People are trying desperately to find their loved ones to communicate with them on the other side. They are beginning to make sacrifices again, using the blood of animals and even the blood of humans to get the other sides' attention. The world has fallen back into the Middle Ages, as people try to understand what is happening and what is going to happen. The noise of confusion and destruction is deafening and heard around the globe. Henry told Nathan he was not to tell anyone else about this.

Now we know those beings are souls being taken to the other side. But what is the other side? Is it heaven or hell, or something else humans haven't even conceived? These are things we must find out before we deliver this new dimension to humans. That was the last entry in Nathan's journal.

In the scientific papers Rick had printed, Lisa found the following. Darkness is not just the absence of light; darkness has its own light waves, we as humans just can't see them. By combining three types of gas Argon, Krypton, and Sulphur Nathan discovered he could see at least one of the blue waves of color in the spectrum. He had mathematical equations for the ratio of each gas and the actual name of the shade of green in the lens. Nathan put in his notes that he wanted to test other gas mixtures with other colored lenses to see if there were other colors in the night spectrum. Nathan developed the lens to give to the scientific community and maybe sell to the military, but mistakenly showed it to his old friend Henry McDavid, who was in Hendersonville. The last thing written by Nathan was, Henry took the lens and had me make eleven more sets, thus making twelve for him. Henry is taking me to a safe place where I can focus on just my work. He wants me to make him a pair of goggles that can be worn, instead of holding the viewer-type lens up to your face.

After reading all the information Rick had found and printed, Lisa knew this whole thing was based on an accidental discovery that, if let out, could destroy the world. It was also based on Henry's greed and willingness to test the portal. Lisa wondered how much money the company had gathered up and was using for Henry's ambition. How many people had followed them over and were now gone.

Lisa had a thought. Why did she need to go back to Hendersonville? Why couldn't she use the lens anywhere? There should be portals all over the place. She grabbed the lens, threw on her shoes and headed out to see if she could find a ragged soul or a portal. She ran into the parking lot and threw the lens up to her face, swinging it back and forth, trying to see something. She was looking far and near, spinning around and turning her head, when she took it down, she realized there were people on the balcony of the hotel watching her. I must look like a crazy person, she thought as she lowered the lens and walked back to her hotel room. She decided to drive out to the outskirts of town to do this. She went back inside, grabbed all of her stuff and threw it in the car. She drove off into the night. When she reached a secluded area on the outskirts of Bakersfield, she stopped the car and got out. She walked a short distance into the darkness and held the lens up to look through. Lisa couldn't believe how well she could see through the lens. It was almost like looking out in the early morning dawn, just before actual daylight, or in the evening at dusk, just before nightfall. This must be the time the different light spectrums meet, and we can still see some of the daylight spectrum as the night spectrum creeps in. Neither spectrum is clear, and the night spectrum disappears into the light of day, while at dusk, the day spectrum disappears into the night, leaving us almost blind in the darkness. Now with this lens, we can see some of the night spectrum, and although we just see gray and blue light and silhouettes of trees and buildings, the other light waves are out there. Lisa spent the next hour or so looking for a lost soul through the lens. Listening for the low rustle of wind to blow. There was nothing, just the occasional dim wavy light way off in the distance. Finally, Lisa got close to one of those wavy, dim blue lights and approached it. She put her hand into it, but there was nothing there, it was just a dim blue light. Lisa got back in the car and drove back to her hotel, where she fell asleep.

The next morning, Lisa gathered up all the stuff she had brought in and packed up her car. She headed to the main road and continued toward Vegas. As she was checking out at a gas station where she bought coffee and something that resembled a sandwich, she had another thought. Why was Hendersonville Tennessee the only place to cross over? Were there other places on Earth to cross over? What was so special about Hendersonville? As Lisa pulled back out on the highway, headed for Vegas, these new questions seemed all she could think about. What if there were other spots on Earth to cross over? Lisa felt like she needed to know the answer to these questions so she could be in complete control of what she was doing. Lisa stopped at a restaurant to grab a bite late in the day as she neared Vegas. She took her laptop in so she could search for some things. Once inside, she turned on her computer and went to the internet. She typed in other dimensions and how they connect with our world. She found very little actual scientific information; it was other dimensions after all. But there was one point that seemed to ring through all the theories she found. That was the straight-line theory. It seemed that in all theories there was a connector from one dimension to the other. Kind of like a spoke on a bicycle tire, all of them are straight, and each one connects the tire to the rim in different places. Hendersonville must be the point that the straight line connects with our world. Lisa read on, some of the theories believe that the straight line goes all the way through the earth and comes out the other side, creating a second point for connection. Lisa did a little calculation and found that a straight line from Hendersonville through the earth would come out in the middle of the Indian Ocean. So, it's just Hendersonville, she thought as she smiled and closed her computer. As Lisa drove on toward Vegas, she was thinking about coming back from the other side. What if I come out in the middle of the ocean, she thought. I should get a small inflatable life raft and add it to my backpack. This made Lisa smile as she drove on toward Vegas.

CHAPTER VI

Exploring

In Vegas, Lisa checked into a cheap hotel and settled in to put a plan together. She started with what she knew about the process. The portals, the souls, and the jewelry. She thought about how she would see the souls come by and follow them to their portal and go through as they did, or just before. On the other side, there were all these buildings, some were open, and some were closed up. The buildings seemed to replicate Hendersonville, and Sarasota on the last trip. She thought about the souls coming after them in their slow movements, even though they were seen as their younger selves, they were moving like they were wandering aimlessly. Lisa realized none of this would help her stay ahead of the company and, hopefully, either eliminate them or take them over. Rick was gone, the only person she felt she could trust. He was gone because he was naïve and trusted someone from his past. His death angered Lisa to the point of wanting revenge on the company, but how? Lisa went to bed that night, considering whether to accept her current situation and live the remainder of her life quietly, sneaking over only when she needed to, leaving the company to its own demise. As Lisa was falling asleep, she remembered what Nathan had said about this discovery and how it would destroy the world. Lisa decided then, and there she had to stop the company and use this discovery to help the world. Though truth be told, she had no idea of how she was going to do either one.

The next morning, Lisa got her answer when she opened one of Rick's computers and saw an email from that same old friend in

Hendersonville. The title was urgent need to talk. Lisa remembered what Rick had told her about phishing emails and how just by opening them people can be tracked and found. This email meant they were looking for her because she knew they had killed Rick. She realized she couldn't stop at this point until the company was gone, or she would be running the rest of her life, or dead. She shut the computer down and got out a pad to write the plan.

She had been successful in getting across to the other side the last time she went over without the company knowing she was there. She knew that with a little tweaking, each time she could get past the company. Now the big thing was getting back once she crossed back over to this side. Could she hire a pilot and put them on a retainer to come wherever she was and bring her home, she thought. That could be the answer to a quick trip over and back. She decided to rent a house there in Vegas under another name and start building for the next visit.

Two weeks later, she had sold all the jewelry and stuff left over from her last trip and used the cash to move into a small house just outside of Vegas, where she set up shop. She bought a new computer and put the accounts and all the information Rick had gathered on it. She burned all the other computers in the backyard and then buried them.

She set about hiring a private jet and a pilot who could be on call when she went across. It turns out that it was easier than she thought it would be. So now she was ready to go back over and see if she could figure out what else was there. She started writing down the questions she needed answers to. The biggest of those questions were based on what Henry had said about there is much more there than just money. Lisa sat there pondering Henry's words. What is there that could be seen as more than money? What else could there be? Lisa was thinking as hard as she could, trying to solve this sort of puzzle she had created for herself. She got up to freshen up her coffee, and as she pushed the power button to turn the coffee maker off it hit her. She remembered those conversations from Key West about power.

"Power, it's got to be power." She said, looking at the coffee maker. Lisa decided she would need to go back over and look around to find out what Henry was talking about. To find the power. This meant finding another follower to go with her and take the stuff while she looked around. She wasn't going to wait for months or even weeks for the relationship to grow this time. She would find someone and get over there as quickly as she could.

She met Danny the next day at a bar, and they started seeing one another. Danny was an ex-police officer, although he was very vague about why he was no longer an officer. He was short and stocky with a round face, not someone Lisa would ever be attracted to normally, but she needed a follower. Things progressed the way they always seemed to, with Danny falling for Lisa. Lisa was going along and saying all the right things to get Danny to go with her. After a couple of days, Lisa felt secure enough in their relationship and told him about the portals, the jewelry, and the trip to the other side. Danny was all in and couldn't wait to go. It wasn't about the money; for Danny, he just wanted the excitement. A week later, they flew to Gallatin, Tennessee, where she had Danny rent a car, while she bought two flexible carry-on bags. They waited till almost nightfall and headed for the outskirts of Hendersonville. Lisa had Danny drive through the city and into that church parking lot, just outside of town, where they waited. Around eleven o'clock, they headed down the road on foot. After a few minutes of walking, Lisa heard a car approaching and pulled Danny off to the side of the road and hid. The car drove slowly by, and Lisa could see four men inside, the company, she thought. They continued down the road to the spot where it had all begun for her and waited just off the road in some trees. Danny was nervous and kept pacing back and forth.

"Stop it." Lisa ordered as she was looking through the lens.

Danny walked over next to her and stood there. Almost an hour had passed before Lisa heard the familiar sound of the wind rustling through the trees.

"Get ready." She told Danny while she was still looking through the lens. Then there she was, being pulled across the road. This soul was heading for the other side. Lisa handed Danny the lens and pointed to where he should look. When Danny saw the lost soul of the woman, he started laughing. Lisa took the lens back and got her bearings by looking through it. Lisa took off following the soul, and Danny was right beside her, still laughing.

"What's so damn funny." Lisa said, almost demanding.

"I don't know, I've never been this scared." Danny admitted as he was working, to stay close to Lisa. Lisa just smiled as she followed the lost soul. They made their way through the woods for about fifty yards, and then Lisa saw the blue light of the sphere.

"There it is." Lisa said, turning to look at Danny. They ran ahead of the soul and pushed their way into it. Once again, Lisa was standing on the other side, looking at the decaying buildings and breathing the ragged, dank air that was here. Danny was stunned by what he saw, and he certainly had stopped laughing. The two of them started walking in the direction they had just come until they were out of the woods. Then they hurried down the street till they saw an open building. They ran inside, and Lisa put Danny on, loading up the bags, while she watched the door. Lisa wanted to explore the city they were in, but now that she was here, she was afraid to just go walking around. She realized she would need a plan to come over here and poke around. She would need to come by herself with a camera and a notepad and keep every piece of information she could gather. She wouldn't worry about the money. She turned to watch Danny. He was scared and was working as fast as he could, just like Lisa had told him to do. Shortly, he had both bags filled, and they took off back the way they had come. They stepped just into the woods to wait for another portal to open. Lisa could see in the light darkness a group of souls coming toward them, and she knew they needed a portal soon. Then, Lisa heard voices and squinted her eyes to see the commotion further down the street.

"Drop the bags and follow me." Lisa whispered as she started walking toward the voices. They walked right past the souls that were walking toward the woods. Lisa started to jog as it seemed to take a long time to get to the building where she heard the voices. Danny was right beside her, staying as close as he could.

"Stay down and behind me." She said in a loud whisper. They seemed to have to run to make any progress toward the men she could see. Finally, they got close enough to see there were four men, three of them were following, carrying two duffel bags each, and one was leading with the lens and giving orders. The crosser not only had the lens, but he was also wearing a gun. A small-caliber handgun on his belt. The four men she had seen in the car just before she and Danny crossed over. In that moment, Lisa had an idea of how she could hurt the company. Lisa waited for them to get out on the street and head toward the woods. She took Danny's hand and ran further into the decaying city. The two of them walked, then ran very briskly down the street toward what Lisa was assuming was the center of town. After they had walked and ran for about ten minutes, Lisa turned to look back on the way they had come. They seemed to be no further away from the woods than before. Lisa stopped and looked all around, wondering what was going on.

"Let's go." Lisa said to Danny as they turned and headed back down the street toward the woods where they had left their bags. They got back to the bags, and Danny grabbed them up. A few minutes later, Lisa found a portal that was close enough, and they started toward it.

"Follow me." Lisa said, now running to stop the feeling of panic that was quickly taking over her mind. As they came to the portal, Lisa pushed Danny straight through it. She followed right behind him. They came out on the other side in a field with short grass. Some kind of pasture, Lisa thought. They knelt, and Lisa took a minute to just breathe and let her mind calm down. Danny was standing up and pointing to something.

"Get down." Lisa snapped as she pulled out her phone to check their location.

"Roosevelt Minnesota?" Lisa said, shaking her head.

"At least we are in the United States." Lisa smiled as she said this. She sent a text to her pilot telling him she was in Roosevelt Minnesota, and asking him to come and get her. International Falls was as close as he could get, and he would be there the next afternoon.

Lisa replied with an ok and the two of them headed out toward the lights in the distance. They shortly found a road and started walking. Danny was carrying both bags and wouldn't let Lisa help him. Once she noticed his strong interest in the jewels, she began to question whether she could trust him. She had never felt like this about any of the other followers. Danny's actions and words made it seem like he would be willing to kill her and take everything for himself. Lisa wasn't sure if her gut feeling was right or if she was just panicked from the crossover. Nonetheless, Lisa decided to always keep Danny in front of her. They found themselves at a small convenience store and went inside. Lisa told Danny she would get them something to eat while he ordered an Uber to take them to International Falls. Danny set about getting it done, while Lisa bought them a roller hotdog and water. Standing inside the store, Lisa was watching Danny as he made a call on his phone. The ride in the car was quiet, and Lisa could see the wheels turning in Danny's head. Was he going to try and take all the money? Lisa thought as she was sitting there beside him in that car. Lisa went on high alert as she realized she could be in danger from Danny.

Later that night at International Falls, Danny used his credit card to rent them a room, and they went inside to sleep. Lisa never really slept in the time she laid there in the darkness, because of the fear she now had of Danny. She got up and sat by the window, thinking about what had happened on the other side. The company was certainly there, and they would be easy to pick off, she thought. That is how I can hurt the company. The bigger question though, was why, after walking for ten minutes, we had not gotten anywhere. It looked like we were walking into town, but when I looked back, we hadn't gone very far at all. It was strange. She also remembered walking right past the souls she thought were coming after her and Danny. They never even acted like they were trying to get us as we walked by them. Lisa gave up and laid her head back in her chair, though she never really slept. The next morning, Lisa was up early and dressed, sitting by the window as Danny slept. When he finally woke up just fine, Lisa was relieved.

"Wow, what a night. What time is it? Danny asked.

"Time to get up and get some breakfast." Lisa said, half smiling. She wondered what Danny was willing to do to keep all the money, and she was on high alert. Who did he call last night, and when will they show up? She thought. She also knew Danny would not make it to breakfast. She let him take his time as she sat there planning her take-down of the company. She would need some things for her next trip over. As she started making her list, she heard the low rustle of wind in the trees, and she knew Danny would be gone in a few minutes. Lisa had grown used to the soul-sucking beings that visited her each time she made a crossing with a follower. So, she barely looked up when this one came for Danny. Lisa looked at her list of things she knew on the left side of the paper and the list of things she didn't know on the right side of the paper. She knew how and where to cross over, and she knew how the lens had been discovered. She knew how to get the jewels back from the other side with no harm to herself. She was certain in the fact that her followers were being taken to a better place, or at least that's what she was going with. She could end up anywhere in the world on her return to this side, but she was now ready for that, she guessed. Lisa thought long about what she knew, trying to see if there was anything she had missed. Lisa let her eyes go to the right side of the paper to the things she didn't know. She didn't know enough about the company to understand how to take it over. She didn't know what other things were on the other side that were better than money. Why were the souls coming toward them? Why couldn't they move forward in the direction of the distant lights? She really didn't know what to do next. Lisa heard the exhale as Danny's soul left his body. She did not even look up to see it leave or see Danny fall back on the bed where he had been sitting, putting his shoes on. Lisa got up to cover his body. That's when she saw the small knife in Danny's hand. He was going to kill me and take the money, the lens and everything. Maybe your soul will remain in this room forever, asshole, Lisa thought. As Lisa covered Danny's body up in the bed and took a moment to gather her stuff, she realized she had never thought about anyone double-crossing her. She would need to be on high alert from now on with her followers. As Lisa walked out of the hotel, she noticed a car in the lot with Nevada tags and a guy leaning against the car smoking. Lisa waited nervously for her Uber to take her to the airport, trying to watch the guy leaning on the car without being noticed. When the Uber pulled up, she quickly loaded the carry-on bags and her backpack and headed to the airport. As she drove away, she smiled because once again she had slipped through the danger she had put herself in.

CHAPTER VII

Team Building

Back in Vegas, she set about developing her plan for the company. Lisa had studied the process with what she knew and didn't know for several days, trying to find a way to either get around the company or destroy it. She concluded she would need to build her own company and either go around or through Henry's company in Hendersonville. One thing was for sure, she would need some help. Lisa went through all the names of her past, trying to pick someone who could help her but also someone she could trust.

Her cousin in Hendersonville was a sheriff's deputy. He would be able to help her build whatever it was she was building. She would have to risk going to Hendersonville, and it would be a risk to even talk to her cousin. He was, after all, a sheriff's deputy, and Henry owned several of the deputies.

Lisa cut and dyed her hair from blond to a light brunette color. She decided to wear big baggie clothes and hoped no one would notice her. Later that day, armed with all her notes and her new computer with all of Rick's stuff on it, she rented a car and headed out from her house in Vegas, driving to Hendersonville. The many hours on the road allowed her to slowly walk through her plan to try and get a person inside the company to give her information. They could let her know when the company was sending crossers over, so she could send her own crossers and hijack them on the other side. If this works, she could send a crosser to ambush them every time. She could take out the company's crossers and convince the poor carriers that they were safer with her. This way, she could increase her income and slow or even stop the income going to the company. This would be risky, she thought, and the people on her team would have to be absolute in their allegiance to her company. That would mean splitting the profits equally and making everyone as important as the others. Her contact in Hendersonville right now was her cousin; she wasn't sure she could trust him, and that worried her. Because if he was crooked, he could take her down. Plus, she didn't really have a backup plan or person. Was there anyone in Hendersonville she could trust with her life? She thought as the night and the road wore on. She decided to stop somewhere in Colorado to sleep and eat. The night was long and quiet in her hotel room, and all Lisa could think about was getting revenge for Rick's death. Or maybe it was all about the money or the excitement of crossing. Whatever it was, it was taking over Lisa's every waking moment. The next morning after breakfast, as she got back on Highway I-forty, she remembered a friend she had as a kid. They went to church together and, for a few summers, were inseparable. Maybe she would be willing to jump into this crazy world. Lisa drove on through the day and finally ended up in Nashville, just south of Hendersonville. Once Lisa was safely in a hotel room, she grabbed her laptop and started searching Facebook for MaryBeth Stevens. It didn't take long before she found her and found out all about her. MaryBeth was divorced with no kids and was now living right here in Nashville. Lisa took a deep breath and sent her an instant message in the hope that she would reply. It only took a few minutes, and MaryBeth said hi back. After a brief conversation that went like this: "Hey, I'm in town. Would you like to meet for dinner to catch up and talk about the old days?" The two women decided to meet, and Lisa was on her way to a local restaurant to meet her old friend. Lisa was sitting in a booth when MaryBeth came walking in. She had aged very well and was a good-looking woman in Lisa's opinion. Her long auburn hair was flowing freely around her smiling face. It was like they were kids again, meeting up after a church softball game for milkshakes, only this time they were adults, and Lisa wasn't interested in milkshakes. After several minutes of small talk as they ate, Lisa finished eating and broke the ice. She had decided to go slow and try to decide about her cousin before reaching out to him.

"Do you remember my cousin Bobby, Bobby Riley? He's a cop now, I think." Lisa asked as innocently as she could.

"Sure do, I used to have the biggest crush on him." MaryBeth said, smiling from ear to ear.

"I need to talk to him about some things." Lisa said. She waited for MaryBeth's reply and report on her cousin and his status in the community and, hopefully, in the company.

"I haven't seen him for a long time, but last I knew he was a preacher at that same little church we grew up in." MaryBeth said, finishing her drink.

"What did you say you do for a living now, MaryBeth?" Lisa asked as she finished her own drink.

"Computer analyst," MaryBeth said.

This was just what Lisa needed to hear, as her last computer analyst was killed.

"We need to talk about some things too, MaryBeth," Lisa said, standing up.

"Okay, we can go back to my house." MaryBeth said, heading out the door. Lisa followed MaryBeth to her little house in the suburbs.

Once in MaryBeth's house, Lisa saw a lot of the same equipment Rick had in his house. So, she knew MaryBeth was a computer whiz too. Lisa decided that she needed to trust someone. MaryBeth was an old friend whom she had trusted all those years ago, and MaryBeth had never broken that trust. So, she began laying out the whole story. MaryBeth was listening intently to every word Lisa told her. There were times Lisa saw disbelief on

MaryBeth's face as she told her everything. Finally, around two in the morning, Lisa was leaving and heading back to her hotel room.

"I'll be at that same diner where we had dinner tonight, at ten in the morning, if you want to be there. If you don't show, then I'll know your decision, and I'll move on." Lisa was as serious as she could be when she left MaryBeth's house. Lisa didn't sleep much that night because she knew if MaryBeth was in with the company, she would be in danger. That's the main reason she never told MaryBeth where she was staying.

The next morning, just before ten, Lisa walked back into the diner, and there sat MaryBeth with a smile as big as the plate her waffle was on. Lisa sat down and just smiled at MaryBeth.

"If you had just waited a minute last night, I would have told you then I'm in." MaryBeth said, looking sternly at Lisa. They sat there in silence, looking up at each other, drinking coffee, and eating waffles; they didn't really talk about the plan at all. After breakfast, they headed back to MaryBeth's house.

"I looked up your cousin Bobby last night." MaryBeth said as she sat down at her computer.

"Don't ever do anything like that again," Lisa said sternly.

"We are in this together, and as I told you last night, it will be dangerous." Lisa explained.

"Ok, I get it." MaryBeth snapped back.

"No, you don't get it. They killed my friend Rick Walker, who had been searching the internet for information on the company. They came to his house and shot him." Lisa was all but crying as she finished.

"I'm sorry, I didn't know that. I knew Rick too. I'll be very careful; it won't happen again." MaryBeth said as she hugged Lisa.

MaryBeth looked concerned as she handed Lisa a piece of paper with all the info on her cousin Bobby she would need to make her decision. The paper read like a glowing endorsement of a human being. Bobby was a senior officer on the police force; he was a leader and teacher, and coached the kids in the community. He did charity work for the homeless, he built houses for humanity, and he volunteered at the pet shelter. Lisa couldn't believe her luck; there was no way this guy was involved with the company. Lisa knew she was going to have to get him out of Hendersonville so she could talk to him safely. She didn't want to put anyone else at risk. Lisa looked through her phone and found her cousin Bobby's old number. She paused, looking at it, running through all the thoughts about what she was about to do. If he wasn't willing to join her, then she could be creating another enemy, and she didn't need that. She slowly touched the number, and her phone went to work. After just a few rings, she heard a familiar voice at the other end; it was her cousin Bobby's voice.

"Well, as I live and breathe, it's my long-lost cousin. "Hi Lisa, how are you?" Bobby said, smiling through the phone.

"I'm good, Bobby." Lisa said, feeling a relief wash over her. Lisa and Bobby spent the next few minutes catching up and laughing about old memories. Finally, Lisa got the courage to ask Bobby to come to Nashville and talk about something very important. Bobby said he would be there the next morning, and they agreed to meet at the diner where Lisa and MaryBeth had met. Lisa and MaryBeth spent the rest of the day making plans for how to set up and run their new company. Lisa did not want to call it a company, as that was what Henry called his business.

"We need a better name for what we're building here." Lisa said, looking at her phone's search engine for words.

"Hey! Remember when we were playing little league softball at church, how we would tell everyone we were in the big league?" MaryBeth blurted out.

"Yes, and that's it; we are now in the league." Lisa said, smiling and nodding.

As the day went on, MaryBeth dug up more information on the company, including finding a list of names. Lisa had her cross-reference those names with obituaries, and they lined up perfectly. All except nine names they weren't dead yet, which meant they had not crossed over.

"There is our marker." Lisa said suddenly.

"If we can find those guys and follow them, we can cross over when they do." When Lisa finished speaking, she noticed MaryBeth was already looking up their addresses. "This is going to work," Lisa thought as she stretched out on the couch. She hadn't felt this relaxed since this all began; she slept well that night.

The next morning, when Bobby walked into the restaurant, it felt like the old days when they were all kids. Bobby had grown into a large man; he stood more than six feet tall and had the physique of an athlete. His arms were large, and his chest and shoulders were thick from all the physical work he did. His smile shone brightly through his mustache as he walked up to Lisa and hugged her. They all sat down and just smiled for a while. All three of them were running through the memories of their childhoods. Then Bobby broke the silence.

"Alright, you said it was important. So, let's get right to it." Bobby said, putting his coffee cup down.

"I don't want to get into the details here, but before we move on, I need you to know that what we're doing is dangerous and people have already died." Lisa finished and sat back, waiting for Bobby's reaction. Bobby just stared at her with an intense stare.

"Any of those dead folks on your hands?" Bobby asked.

"I have not killed anyone if that's what you're asking. I am trying to take down something called the company in Hendersonville." Lisa said, staring straight at Bobby.

"The company?" Bobby leaned forward and whispered. "What do you know about the company?"

"Quite a lot, as it turns out." MaryBeth chimed in, smirking.

"Let's go to MaryBeth's place so we can talk." Lisa said, throwing some money on the table.

The three of them left and headed to MaryBeth's house. Once inside, Lisa began to explain everything because she felt like Bobby could see right through her. Lisa started with the lens. She explained how it came to be, how Henry McDavid had hijacked it, and how Nathan Ashton was nowhere to be found. She went on to explain the portals and crossing over to the other side. How she would take a follower with her to grab the money, and the soul takers would come for them in the next day or so. She even told Bobby about what Henry had told her about there being much more than just money over there. After a couple of hours of discussions, Bobby had more questions than Lisa had answers to. He decided to leave and come back the next day. Bobby needed some time to process what he had just learned.

After Bobby left, MaryBeth found an interesting post on one of the carrier's Facebook posts. It basically said tonight is the night that will change my life. I'll see you on the other side.

Lisa asked MaryBeth if she could get a gun. MaryBeth walked to the bedroom and came back with two Glock pistols and an extra clip for both. She handed one to Lisa and smiled. As Lisa put the gun in her backpack, she asked MaryBeth if she wanted to cross over with her tonight. MaryBeth was already standing in the door waiting for Lisa. Lisa was putting the plan together as the two of them took an Uber to the back roads of Hendersonville.

Lisa sent Bobby a text and said they were going to crossover and see if they could hijack the companies' men. They would be back in town in a few days; she would reach out when they got back. Lisa added, "Please do not trust or tell anyone about what we're doing."

The two women walked down the road to where Lisa and Tim had first crossed; they stepped off into the woods and waited. Bobby texted back, asking them to wait for him. Lisa told him it was too late; the company men would be here soon. She added, "Just be prepared when we get back to save the world, and don't trust anyone." About eleven o'clock, a car slowly pulled up and stopped just short of where the girls were hiding. Lisa turned to MaryBeth and smiled as they got ready.

"Remember, we have to go in the same place they go to, so we have to be right behind them." Lisa said as she pulled out the lens.

"Also, do not touch any of the jewelry or gems lying around on the ground." Lisa glanced at Marybeth sideways, not wanting to lose sight of the lens as she finished her warning. There was one crosser; he had the lens. There were three followers, each of whom had two bags with them, and they were waiting to follow the crosser to the other side. Lisa noticed they had made the lenses into goggles, and he was wearing them like skiing goggles. When the four men took off, so did Lisa and MaryBeth; they were staying very close to the men but trying not to be noticed. Lisa was looking through her lens to try and see where they were going; MaryBeth was just trying to keep up with Lisa. After a couple of minutes, they saw the portal and the crosser, and the carriers sped up past the soul. They went through just before the soul started being sucked into the portal. Lisa grabbed MaryBeth's hand and dragged her through as the soul went through. On the other side, the men were already several feet ahead of them and running at full speed back the way they had come. Lisa and MaryBeth took off running after them. The four men were so focused on where they were going and what they were doing, they never had a clue that Lisa and MaryBeth were right behind them. The decayed city came upon them very quickly, and they found themselves standing in the middle of the street as the four men ran and kicked their way into a closed building to stuff their bags full of loot. Lisa and MaryBeth crept to the door and waited just outside; Lisa wasn't sure about what her next move would be. MaryBeth took a minute to take in what she was seeing and couldn't believe it or make any sense out of it. She looked all around the ground and could see handfuls of rings and bracelets lying everywhere. MaryBeth remembered what Lisa had told her about even touching the jewelry, so she put it out of her mind and focused on the door the company men had run into. As they stood there, Lisa put the lens up to her eyes to see what she could see. Looking through the lens, she could see the town in a different light. It was beautiful and vibrant. The day was gray; there were people walking and talking just like in her world. She jerked the lens down and blinked her eyes; now the same things were rotten and decaying. She put the lens back up and looked through it again. Through all the trips to this side of the grave, she had always looked through the lens in the woods to find a portal and had not taken a moment to look at this world. She was always almost in a panic; she had never looked in this direction before or realized what she was seeing. This was something new for her to process and figure out. Did Henry know about this? Was this what he meant about something more over here? MaryBeth gave Lisa a light shove to bring her back to the moment. Lisa saw the men coming out of the building. The followers were in front, and the crosser was behind them, carrying his goggles. When the crosser stepped in front of Lisa, she held out the gun and stopped the crosser. The crosser paused and looked at her, then went to take out his own gun. A shot rang out, and the crosser went down to his knees as the blood filled in his shirt. Lisa looked up to see MaryBeth pointing the gun. MaryBeth gave Lisa a smirk and nod as she turned her gun to the followers. They just stood there frozen, looking at the dead crosser. Lisa heard the light rustling of wind in the trees; she threw her lens up to her eyes, and she saw the soul of the crosser rise and begin to walk away. That was fast, she thought as she grabbed the goggles from his hand and motioned the followers toward the way they had come in. As they walked briskly toward the outskirts of town, she asked one of the followers what they were getting paid for doing this. They all looked at her, and one held up a bag of jewelry. Lisa realized they are told they get one of the two bags they carry back.

"Same deal, follow me." Lisa said, leading them into the woods. They waited for a portal to open close to them because now there were five of them going back through. Lisa told the followers and MaryBeth that they all had to get back through the portal at the same time, or they would be lost forever; don't hesitate. At last, a portal opened up close enough. Lisa ran toward it with the others right behind her. Lisa came out on the other side into water that was knee deep. As the others came running through, Lisa was trying to get an idea of where they were. Lisa realized it was a small stream and started heading to the bank. Out of the water, she pointed her gun at the followers and told them to sit down and wait for her instructions. MaryBeth already had her phone out and had located their position.

"We're just outside of Scobey, Montana." MaryBeth said, looking at Lisa like a little girl asking how we are going to get home.

"Well, at least we're in the United States." Lisa said, smiling.

Lisa took out her phone and pulled up the compass. They needed to head southeast toward town.

"Let's go," Lisa said, still waving the gun. As the five of them started walking downstream toward town, Lisa was thinking about how best to handle the two extra bags tomorrow after the demise of the followers. While she was going through all this, she had another thought. The company can't find the bodies of the followers, or they will know what has happened. So, Lisa decided to stop where they were, back in these foothills. Lisa stopped the group and told them she had a car and a plane to get them home, but not until tomorrow. They would be hard-pressed to explain why they are way out here with six bags of loot if they go on into town. The followers all agreed, and they all settled in for the last couple of hours of night. Lisa didn't sleep, as she was thinking about what she had seen through the lens and what it meant. As the morning broke and the sun started rising, Lisa was anxious about the soul catchers coming, as she knew the three men would grow restless waiting simply because she said to wait. Lisa devised a story and told the followers that it would take about a day and a half for her team to get to them and that they needed to stay where they were until then, so they didn't raise a fuss in town. The three men agreed and settled in, each one holding his bag close. Later that same day, as the afternoon was cooling down toward nightfall, Lisa heard the familiar sound of rustling wind in the trees. She looked at the three men, and they were sitting and staring, unable to move or speak. When MaryBeth saw the beings through the goggles, she jumped up and ran behind a tree; from there, she watched the soul catchers take the last breath from the men and their souls rise and begin their journey back to the other side. Lisa looked at MaryBeth and motioned to the bodies. The women used their hands and sticks to dig a shallow grave and roll the men's bodies into it. They covered the bodies with loose dirt, leaves, sticks, and rocks. Lisa tied two of the bags together, and they would each carry one bag and pull the other two bags as they started off toward town. Lisa pulled out her phone and sent a message to her pilot telling him where they were. Glasco was the closest airport, and he could be there the next day.

"We have to get to a road." Lisa said as the two women headed out.

It was well past dark when they found a road. Lisa pulled out her phone and ordered an Uber. Thirty minutes later, they were on their way to Glasco. In the hotel in Glasco, Lisa started trying to tell MaryBeth about what she had seen on the other side through the lens. She wasn't sure what she saw, so she was having trouble describing it. MaryBeth listened carefully and was trying to process what she heard. Exhausted, the two women fell asleep trying to figure it out. The next morning, they found a small restaurant near the airport and went inside. Once again, Lisa was trying to figure out what she had seen through the lens and what it meant; she had no idea. Around noon, they were finally on the plane and headed back to Nashville. In Nashville, they took an Uber back to MaryBeth's place, where they collapsed on the couch. After a few minutes, MaryBeth couldn't wait any longer and opened one of the suitcases. It was stuffed full of rings, necklaces, brooches, and other trinkets; all six cases were stuffed full of the stuff. MaryBeth couldn't believe all this loot. While Lisa was certain her plan would work and she would be able to control this, whatever this was, the two women just looked at one another and smiled.

"I killed a guy." MaryBeth said in a concerned voice.

"Yes, but it was in another world, and he was a bad guy, so it doesn't count." Lisa said, smiling.

"Well, okay then." Marybeth said as she took her shirt off and headed for the shower.

The next day, Lisa reached out to Bobby and told him they were back. While they waited for him to get there, MaryBeth was busy going through the jewelry and preparing piles to be taken and sold. Then she would deposit the money into the accounts she had set up for herself and Lisa.

When Bobby got there the next morning, he was very nervous and seemed distracted. He pulled out a little notebook and started reviewing the notes he had written inside.

"Look, I'm not sure what you two are up to, but I don't think you know who you're dealing with." Bobby said, holding his little notebook up.

"Henry McDavid," Lisa said, looking at Bobby.

"We've done some research and know quite a lot about him and his company." MaryBeth said, typing away at her keyboard.

"That's great that you know his name. Do you also know that over one hundred people have gone missing just in the Hendersonville area?" Bobby snorted back.

"Do you remember Rick Walker?" Lisa snapped back at Bobby.

"Yes, he was that geeky guy you dated for a bit," Bobby replied.

"They shot him on his front porch, Bobby. Because he was looking into the company for me." Lisa said, with her eyes filling up with tears.

Bobby turned around and stared out the window for a minute to gather his thoughts.

"My partner started working with them. He left one night, bragging about how his life was going to change forever. I never saw him again; he was just gone, with no trace; he was just gone." Bobby realized he had raised his voice as he finished. He stepped back and took a deep breath.

"So, we both have a reason to take out the company." Lisa said calmly.

"Don't forget these reasons." MaryBeth said, pulling the bed sheet back on nine piles of jewelry.

Lisa spent the rest of the day explaining the whole process to Bobby. That explanation included that Bobby's partner was probably a follower, and his soul was taken back to the other side. She also told Bobby about what she had seen through the lens on the other side. It was still something she would need to figure out. As the three of them headed out for dinner, all the cards were on the table; everyone knew what going ahead with this meant, people would die, and they would be in grave danger.

CHAPTER VIII

Recon

The trio decided to pack up and head back to Lisa's place in Vegas and use it as their headquarters so they would be far away from the company. They loaded all MaryBeth's equipment and a few of her personal things into a truck. Bobby showed up that morning with two boxes and a go bag. The three of them left headed for Vegas. The drive was long, and everyone seemed to be on the edge of breaking down or screaming at the others. They all rode in silence, each one pondering what the hell they were doing. Lisa knew she now had a team and could move on to the company, but the how and when was still unknown. Once back in Vegas at Lisa's house, they set about setting up the league. MaryBeth set up all her computer equipment in one room, Lisa had maps spread out covering the table in the dining room, and then there was the money room where they had stashed all the suitcases from the last trip over. MaryBeth set up accounts with Lisa, herself, and Bobby's name on them. She took several piles of jewelry and headed off to find a fence where she could sell it. When she came back with money in hand, she counted out a few thousand for them to split. She then headed out to the local banks and started dumping money into the accounts. There didn't seem to be a problem with depositing small amounts of money through the banks. Bobby and Lisa were going through the maps, notes, and all the information they had.

"We need a plan." Bobby said looking over the maps.

"But first we need to figure out what we are trying to do." Lisa said, not looking up.

When they put their minds into what outcome they wanted from all of this, it was the same for all, take out Henry McDavid and take over the company. Just then, MaryBeth came loudly through the door carrying lunch for everyone. They all gathered around the sink to eat, as it was the last open space in the kitchen.

"Once we have control with the league and it's our money, then we start giving the money to organizations that can help the poor." Bobby said smiling.

"Wow, donations to charitable organizations." That's a great way to use this money. Why didn't I think of that?" MaryBeth said as she rolled her eyes.

"No, I'm not talking about laundering the money. I mean, give the money to people in need, help humanity with this." Bobby replied sternly. Lisa and MaryBeth smiled and nodded.

The three of them worked for the next week on creating a plan that would eventually end up with them in charge of this whole thing, and they would use the money and any power the league gained for good.

The plan started with Bobby going back to Hendersonville and quietly gathering as much information as he could on the company. As a cop, he would be able to look at old police cases and talk to people Lisa would never be able to approach. Lisa would bounce back and forth between Nashville and Vegas, gathering information about the remote areas where the crossings took place. She was also trying to figure out what more was in the other dimension that was so important to Henry. MaryBeth was going to monitor the list of people she had flagged for followers and try and find the next crossing date. Lisa and Bobby hopped on a plane back to Nashville. Bobby went home, and Lisa went to MaryBeth's house. The next day, back at the police station, Bobby started looking into crimes and information that included the company or Henry McDavid. What he found was startling, in that a lot of things were left out of cases, or the files were just gone. Bobby knew that meant there were some of Henry's men on the force, and he would have to be even more careful. After looking through a big stack of case files all, he had on the company was a few ghost-like glimpses and mentions. Bobby decided not to dig any deeper here in the police station or directly into police files for fear of giving himself and the league away. He was going to get the names of the followers that were left and start watching them, to see if they led him to anyone higher up in the force. Lisa found a series of hollers in the foothills that seemed to funnel into one specific area. The place in the woods where the hollers came together created a circular area. From satellite photos, the area looked like a big circle with the ridges making it look like spokes on a wheel. So maybe that was why Hendersonville was the epicenter of the crossings, although she was sure there were similar hollers and ridges all over the world. Maybe it was what she originally thought from her limited online searches, and it's just where the portal from the other side came out on our side, so that made it the epicenter. Meanwhile, at the same time, MaryBeth was looking into the reason Hendersonville was the epicenter too, she found that if you look at the earth as a globe and mark a spot as the center of the earth, it is nowhere near Hendersonville. She drew a line straight through the earth from Hendersonville it came out in the middle of the Indian ocean like Lisa had told her. So, she was just as confused about it as she was when she started her search.

The league was coming together and getting ready to make its move on the company. Lisa was looking for Bobby to come up with a plan for the takeover. Bobby had been surveilling people and putting together his plan. MaryBeth was building profiles on every member of the company she could identify. She was monitoring their movements on the internet through social media. It was this monitoring that gave a big clue to the next crossover. MaryBeth got three message alerts all within a couple of minutes of each other. Telling the followers to come to the warehouse tonight at nine o'clock to begin their journey to change their lives. When MaryBeth sent these messages to Lisa, she wasn't sure what Lisa would do with them. Lisa could not help herself when she saw the messages because she wanted to go back over, part of her needed to go back over, so she reached out to Bobby and told him where to meet her that night, just outside of Hendersonville. When the car dropped Lisa off at the church a mile or so from where they would lay in wait, she was relieved to see Bobby sitting on the steps. Lisa took her backpack off and sat down next to Bobby.

"When we get there, and we start moving, don't question what I say and above all, keep up." Lisa finished talking and handed Bobby the viewfinder she had been using; she would be wearing the goggles from the last trip. Well, after dark the two of them headed down the road, being ever so aware of cars and getting out of sight when one came by. They made it to Lisa's waiting place just a few minutes before the company guys pulled up. There were four men against one crosser, and three followers; all three followers had two bags. Both groups waited patiently for the next poor soul to come dragging by. It took a while before a woman slowly appeared, and the company guys took off after her. Lisa and Bobby followed as close as they could. As they approached the blue sphere of light, the company guys ran through before the soul got there. Lisa and Bobby had to go through at the same time, as the soul. It was still as weird a feeling as the first time Lisa had gone through, she thought. On the other side, Lisa came out and just started walking several feet behind the company guys. She had gone a little way when she realized Bobby wasn't right behind her.

"Hey." She whispered loudly as she was motioning for Bobby to come on. Bobby quickly fell out of his trance and hurried to catch up to Lisa. They followed the company guys right up to the doorway of a building; there, they waited just outside. Lisa took the opportunity to use the goggles to study the world on this side. It looked so much like the world on her side as long as she was looking through the goggles. She looked all around but didn't come to any conclusions about what or where this world was, or what the souls on this side were doing. After several minutes and listening to one of the followers yelling and celebrating, all four men started out. The crosser was behind the three followers as before, so when the crosser stepped out, Lisa stuck her gun in his face. The guy stopped and looked like he had seen a ghost. The color drained out of his face, and he just stood there staring at Lisa. Bobby came up behind him and snatched his gun out of his beltline. The crosser slowly raised his arms and stood there. The three followers had stopped as well and were standing just watching. Bobby took out his handcuffs and put them on one wrist of the crosser. He snapped the other end around a metal gate post. Lisa took the lens goggles out of his hand and turned toward the followers. She waved her Glock in the direction of the way they had all come in.

"Please don't leave me here." The crosser begged.

Bobby looked at Lisa, and they started to move down the street. As they left the streets of town and started into the ragged woods, they could hear the screams of the crosser they had left behind. He was begging for them to come back and get him. Lisa turned and looked through the lens to see if any of the souls responded to the screams, but they did not. They just continued on with their wondering about. He was screaming and crying historically until they heard a gunshot, and he stopped screaming, then there was just silence again. Bobby knew he had made a mistake by not searching the guy. He looked at Lisa and shook his head. As the five of them stood there waiting for the next portal, Lisa looked at Bobby and nodded, knowing that now he understood the whole thing.

"We'll give you the same deal as the company." Lisa told the three followers.

"Just stay close so we all make it back. When I say go, don't hesitate, just go." Lisa was talking to Bobby as much as she was talking to the three followers. Lisa noticed Bobby staring at all the jewelry lying around on the ground. "Don't even think about it." Lisa growled. Shortly, a portal opened up near enough for them all to make it through.

"Run." That was all Lisa said as she took off.

The five of them came running through the portal, and two of the followers went tumbling as their legs couldn't keep up with their momentum.

When the commotion stopped, Lisa looked around. It was a desert; they were in a desert. She grabbed her phone, and her heart dropped as she realized she had no service. She looked at Bobby who was looking around himself, realizing they were in a desert.

"What now?" Bobby snapped, waving his gun at the followers, making them all sit down.

"We wait till daylight and try to figure out which way to go. We will only have one chance at getting out of here, so we have to make it count." Lisa said as she plopped down on the still warm sand. After a few hours, the sky began to lighten, and Lisa knew it wouldn't be long until the sun was sucking the life out of them. In the pale morning light, Bobby saw some large rocks in the distance.

"Let's try and get to those rocks for shade." He said, motioning to the followers to get up and start moving. Lisa didn't argue and just fell in behind them, walking toward the rocks. The rocks were farther away than they realized, and it took several hours to get there, but there was indeed some shade that they all crammed into. The day wore on, and the temperature rose with every passing increment of time. In the late afternoon, one of the followers suddenly jumped up, grabbed one of the bags and started running. Bobby jumped up to stop him, but Lisa waved at him to stop. The man only made it a little way before the loose sand tripped him up, and he fell; he just laid there breathing heavily. Shortly, Lisa heard the familiar rustle in the wind in the trees. She could still see the follower who had run in the distance. He had set up and was still now. Lisa watched as his body fell over. She turned her attention to the two followers who were left, and they were slumping, unable to talk or move. Their bodies fell back as the soul catchers took the two followers' souls, leaving their bodies to become part of this desert. Lisa and Bobby were at a loss for what to do. As the sun set, and the day was turning into night, Bobby knew they had to come up with a plan soon, or they would just die out here with the followers. They both knew that really their only chance was MaryBeth getting to them. They sat there with the weight of this fact on both of their minds. Suddenly, in the last glimpses of daylight, there was a thumping sound in the distance. Bobby knew it could be a helicopter. Just as he was realizing this, Lisa yelled. "Look at a helicopter!" They both stood there watching as it approached, never really thinking it could be the company guys. The chopper came right to them and hovered as it lowered a basket down. Lisa took three of the bags and climbed into the basket. She was taken straight up and into the helicopter. Bobby watched from the ground as the basket came back down for him. He threw the last three bags in and jumped in. When he got to the helicopter platform, he could see Lisa drinking from a large water bottle. He climbed out of the basket and strapped himself in as the chopper took off, flying back to where it had come from. Lisa was looking at her phone as they landed in a small airfield on the outskirts of a small town in Egypt.

From there, they were driven to the other side of the airfield to the familiar sight of Lisa's pilot and plane. Lisa was so relieved to see that plane that she started to cry with joy. Bobby grabbed most of the bags, and Lisa grabbed the rest. They shoved them into the small plane and closed the door behind themselves.

"Las Vegas!" was all Lisa said as she and Bobby fell into the seats on the small plane. A few minutes later, they were on their way. Lisa was wondering how in the world the helicopter had found them. She couldn't understand it at all. She looked at Bobby, but he was already asleep. She took out her phone to see if she had any signal, and she did. She put in a FaceTime call to MaryBeth to check in. When MaryBeth came on, she was smiling from ear to ear.

"Well, it's good to know the air tags work, even in the desert." MaryBeth said, still smiling.

"What air tag?" Lisa asked, halfway smiling back.

"The air tag I put in your backpack. That I couldn't tell you about because you were too focused on the company." MaryBeth answered, still smiling from ear to ear.

"Thank you, thank you." Lisa said, smiling back now.

"We'll see you in about thirteen hours." Lisa said, signing off the call. Lisa laid her seat back and fell asleep.

When Lisa woke up, Bobby was sitting across from her, drinking coffee. Lisa dragged herself up and headed to the bathroom. When she came out, Bobby had fixed her a cup of coffee and was holding it out for her. She took the coffee and sat back down.

"So now I know what you meant when you said you haven't actually killed anyone." Bobby said.

"Yea I just let nature take its course." Lisa said.

Lisa notices Bobby's notebook is open on the table. About halfway down the page, she saw the name Nathan Ashton, with a question mark beside it.

"What about Nathan?" She asked, sipping on her coffee.

"That's the guy the entire police force is looking for right now." Bobby said, looking at Lisa.

"That's the scientist who invented the lens. If he is alive, we must find him." Lisa said.

"How did MaryBeth find us?" Bobby asked.

"She put an air tag in my backpack." Lisa said, smiling. Suddenly, they both had a realization that there could be air tags in the suitcases they had just hijacked. They both jumped up and started going through the bags. Each bag had an air tag in it. Bobby grabbed them all and twisted the backs off, removing the battery and shutting them down. Lisa thought about the first six bags she and MaryBeth had taken. Did they have air tags in them? If so, they could lead the company straight to Lisa's house.

"What about the other bags me and MaryBeth took?" Lisa asked Bobby.

"If they have air tags, they will lead the company straight to the house." Lisa said as she was calling MaryBeth with FaceTime. When MaryBeth answered the FaceTime call, Lisa didn't waste a second. She told MaryBeth to go check the bags they had brought back from their crossing. MaryBeth didn't hesitate, she jumped up and ran to the room where those bags were stored.

"What am I looking for?" MaryBeth asked, almost panicking.

"Air tags or any tracking device." Bobby yelled at the screen. MaryBeth pulled each bag out and went through it completely, sticking her hands in all the pockets and pouches. There were no tags or anything in the bags.

"They had no reason to put air tags in the bags before you two struck." Bobby said.

"They probably put one on the crosser as I did with you." MaryBeth said as she walked back into the main room of the house.

"The company would've already been there if they had tagged those bags." Bobby said.

"Alright, so the ones we found in these bags are the first ones the company has used." Lisa said, relaxing a bit.

Now they just had to be aware when they landed in case someone was waiting. They closed the FaceTime call, sat back down relieved, then Bobby got up and went to the pilot.

"We need you to take us to a secluded part of the airport to let us out." Bobby told the pilot. The pilot just nodded.

The two of them rode the rest of the way home without talking much, but there was a lot going on under the surface as each one was planning what to do if Henry's men were waiting on them. Lisa called MaryBeth and told her to wait in the cell phone lot until they called her and told her where to come to. The small plane taxied into a back lot and stopped next to a hanger. The pilot motioned toward a side door, and that's where Bobby and Lisa went. From there, they made it out to the street and called MaryBeth. They stood there looking around nervously until Marybeth came speeding up in the car. They loaded up quickly and drove away. They never actually saw any of the company men, but that was certainly a close call.

Once back in Las Vegas and in Lisa's house, they had time to reflect on what had just happened. Bobby was planning on going back to Hendersonville to look for Nathan, and he told Lisa that it was going to be his focus.

Nathan, Ashton? MaryBeth asked, opening her computer.

"Yes." Bobby said, packing up his travel bag.

"I think I may have an address for you Bobby." Marybeth was smiling as she told Bobby.

Bobby and Lisa turned and just looked at her.

"Yes, it's right here. Rick found a second address for Nathan when he was gathering info on him. MaryBeth finished talking and turned to the printer. The printer spit out a piece of paper, and she handed it to Bobby.

"That's Paducah Kentucky." Bobby said, smiling at Lisa.

"Come on, let's go Bobby." Lisa said, grabbing her backpack.

Bobby knew they needed to strike and finish the company, or they would end up fighting on the company's terms, and that could prove difficult, if not impossible. Lisa just wanted Henry McDavid to be gone, as she had grown to hate him.

CHAPTER IX

Nathan Ashton

Lisa was nervous as she and Bobby walked through the Paducah, Kentucky airport. She knew they could find the address easily enough. But what if the company was already there? What if Nathan didn't want any part of this? Lisa looked at Bobby and smiled confidently while her brain was spinning like a top. As they climbed into the rental car, Lisa got the file out that MaryBeth had given her with a picture. So, they would know who they were looking for. The file also included some information about Nathan and his invention that could help them convince Nathan. As they headed down the street, Lisa suggested they find a small restaurant and grab a bite to eat and talk about their plan to get Nathan to come along with them. Bobby agreed, and they turned into the first place they found. They ordered their food and sat quietly waiting for it to come out. Lisa broke the silence with a joke.

"Maybe we should've ordered hotdogs." Lisa said, giggling. Bobby just stared at her, never cracking a smile.

"You see the connection right, Nathan. Nathan's hotdogs been around... forever." Lisa was waving her hand as she finished talking. Bobby was fixated on how they were going to approach Nathan when they found him.

"We have to get him alone in our car or alone in the house. We may even have to force him to..." Bobby finished abruptly as the waitress arrived with their food. The waitress just smiled and set their food down. After she walked away, Bobby looked very serious at Lisa.

"We'll figure it out. Now eat." Lisa said as she dug into her food.

After dinner, they headed toward the address they had for Nathan. Driving along the side streets in Paducah, Bobby was careful not to draw attention to them. It didn't take long till they were driving by the house at the address. Bobby parked the car half a block down the street, and the two of them just sat there waiting for the other one to say what to do. It was getting dark, and Bobby wanted to approach Nathan before dark if they could, as the daylight seemed to make people feel better about a stranger knocking on their door. Lisa was looking at the cars parked along the street to see if any of them seemed suspicious. Finally, Bobby came up with a plan.

"I'll go first and get in the backyard. You knock on the front door and try to convince him we're here to help." Bobby said, shaking his head. "If he runs, I'll be waiting to stop him." Bobby finished and looked at Lisa. Lisa just nodded and opened her door. The two of them started walking toward the house, and Bobby cut through a couple of houses to get to the back. Lisa paused for a minute, looking around like she was lost, then proceeded to the house. Lisa took a deep breath, stepped up to the door and knocked. After a long pause of silence, she knocked again, this time with a little more force.

"Who..., is it?" She heard Nathan ask from inside.

"My name is Lisa Riley, Nathan, and I'm here to help." Lisa had stepped up close to the door, so she didn't have to yell as loud.

"Lisa Riley!" Nathan said as he started to unlock the door from the inside. Nathan opened the door and motioned Lisa in. Lisa was expecting a small, nerdy, geek-like guy, but Nathan was tall with dark hair and quite muscular. Lisa smiled as she walked in, and Nathan locked the door behind her.

"Let me get my partner from the backyard." Lisa said, walking through the house. She opened the back door and motioned Bobby in. Bobby introduced himself to Nathan and smiled.

"Glad you didn't come running out the back, one of us would've got hurt." Bobby said smiling.

The three of them sat down at Nathan's kitchen table, and Lisa took out the notes she had from Rick and a pad to take more notes.

"How did you find me?" Nathan asked, staring at Lisa.

"My friend Rick was very good at finding information on the internet. But Henry and his company killed him in cold blood." Lisa said, looking back at Nathan.

"We have a lot of questions for you." Bobby said to get started. Lisa had a different idea about the whole process. If they could get Nathan to come with them and join their team, it would be safer for Nathan and for them. Lisa started talking before Bobby could ask the first question.

"Look, right now, right here, we are all sitting here with our asses hanging out in the wind. If we could find you, it's only a matter of time till the company does too." Lisa stated matter-of-factly.

"Nathan, come with us. Our goal is to use this for the good of all humanity, and the good of the planet." Lisa finished with her eyes fixed on Nathan. Bobby could see that Nathan was thinking about everything, so he decided to throw it in with Lisa.

"Nathan, I'm a Hendersonville cop, not on the company's payroll. I can assure you that what Lisa is telling you is true. We need you and your expertise to help us with this. But she's right, we need to get out of here." Bobby finished talking and nodded to Lisa. Nathan sat there staring at Lisa, then stood up and walked across the kitchen to the sink, where he leaned on it heavily. He slowly began to nod his head; he raised up and looked at the two of them.

"Let me get my stuff." Nathan said, turning toward the hallway.

The three of them worked quickly to put Nathan's papers and files in some boxes, his computer and all his materials. There was a small gate in the back leading into the backyard. Bobby used the cover of darkness to pull the car around and through the gate so they could load it up. As they were leaving Paducah, Nathan knew he was with the right people now, and he knew he could help.

The drive from Paducah to Vegas was about 24 hours, so the three of them decided to take turns driving so they could go straight through. Lisa took the last leg of the drive, so she sat in the back of the car. She felt safe with Bobby and Nathan. For the first time since this all began, she finally had people she could trust, and she dozed off until it was her turn to drive. While she was dozing, Bobby told Nathan what they were planning for the company. Nathan was all for it as he had grown to hate Henry as well. Nathan told Bobby he was very happy they had come when they did because he was running out of options.

Back in Vegas, Bobby took the rental car back. Lisa and MaryBeth helped Nathan get settled in the garage with all his stuff. It was late, and the day had been long, and they had been traveling forever, it seemed. Lisa announced she was going to sleep, and everyone should get some rest. Lisa had trouble falling asleep, though, as the fight that was coming loomed heavy on her mind. She did finally go to sleep, and she slept deeply for the first time in a long time.

The next morning, Bobby was up first, and Lisa was up shortly after. As they drank their coffee, the two of them discussed what they needed from Nathan so they could move on to the company. They decided they needed three pieces of information. Number one was what else was over there besides money. Number two, how big the company was, and were there other organizations involved. And number three, how could they best attack the company to end it or take it over? Lisa looked at the small list she had jotted down, nodded and got up to get some more coffee. Nathan came into the kitchen a little later and poured himself a cup of coffee. He sat down, looked at Lisa and smiled.

"I haven't slept that good in months." He spoke. "I feel like I've been given redemption, and I have some control again." He spoke with clarity in his voice. Lisa told Nathan they needed some information, and they hoped he had it.

"Let's start with what else is on the other side, other than jewelry?" Lisa spoke as she turned to a clean page in her notebook. Nathan smiled and began; he talked about what Henry really wanted from the other side. He wants the power to control who is taken from this world. Henry believes he can find that over there, and with it, he can control this world. He went on. Right now, if there is a being that controls the other side, it only takes the dead from this world randomly and of course, now the ones who dare to take from that realm, the followers, if you will. Henry is not sure what the thing on the other side is, as he has never actually seen it. But he believes something over there is making decisions about these things. Why else do people seem to die here when they have everything to live for, Henry believes they are taken by some force, and nothing is random. When Henry started talking about control of the other side, that was the moment, I knew I was in trouble. Nathan went on. Imagine if you could decide who lives and who dies in this world, you could force people to do your bidding; you could put the leaders you want in influential posts around the world. We're talking about world domination here. That's when I started planning my getaway.

"How big is the company?" Lisa asked as she was scribbling on her note page.

"I'm not sure. I believe it's just what Henry has built there in Hendersonville with the police and a couple of local banks. He has several businesses on his payroll too, to help with fencing the stuff they bring back and to keep an eye open for any possible threats. I know he is pulling his followers in from around the country, so people won't get suspicious of all the missing people there in Hendersonville.

"Your police chief's idea." Nathan said, smirking at Bobby.

"Henry is small-minded and greedy." "He understands this discovery could change the world as we know it, maybe even destroy it, but he is reckless with it because of his own greed." Nathan finished talking and looked into his coffee cup.

"I found a list of a few more than a hundred missing people, I believe could be tied to the company. How many more do you think are missing from around the country, or world?" Bobby asked.

"I really don't know, but a lot, I'd say. They usually take three with them when they crossover, and they crossover all they can" Nathan said.

"How can we end Henry and his company?" Bobby asked, standing up, to get another cup of coffee.

"Henry is holed up in an old house somewhere on the Cumberland River. He only comes out when they are crossing over, or when he feels threatened, like when he came and met you and that guy at the diner. That's how I knew your name the other day. Henry is obsessed with you. Said he was going to get you to come and join him on this." Nathan said, stirring his coffee. That piece of information sent chills down Lisa's spine, because she realized that's why Henry hadn't killed her.

"So, Henry's been following me?" Lisa asked firmly.

"Yes, he's had your place in Sarasota staked out now for weeks, just waiting for you to come back. He wanted to grab you and convince you to join him, or kill you, either one would work for him. Not exactly sure how he would decide, it probably depended on whether you joined him or not." Nathan spoke as if this was the way things were.

"Do you know where this house is in Hendersonville?" Bobby asked.

"I can't give you the address, but I was there a couple of times, so I could show you if we were there." Nathan said, drinking the last of his coffee.

Get on Google Earth and see if you can pinpoint it for us. You are too valuable to take back to Hendersonville." Bobby said nodding.

Nathan went on to explain everything to Lisa and Bobby about the lens. He explained that the lens sees night light over here, but only one wavelength, blue, therefore, we only see silhouettes with a little detail on this side. He hasn't discovered the right gas mixture and exact color of the lens to see other colors on the spectrum of the night light on this side. He doesn't even know what colors are on the night light spectrum yet. But on the other side, it turns the night light waves into colorful scenes, and you can see things that you wouldn't be able to see there without the lens. He went on, if you look through the lens in the daytime here on this side, you can only see blurred colors, it's like looking through a piece of frosted glass, kind of like a photo that's way out of focus. The lens only works on dark light waves. Now that we know they exist, we must study them to fully understand them. Nathan paused and looked out the window. Lisa asked Nathan about the experiment he and Henry had done at the hospice house with the dying person. "How do you know about that?" Nathan asked, shaking his head.

"You put it in your journal on your computer, so my, our friend Rick found it, and he printed it out for me before he was killed." Lisa told him. Nathan shook his head and stared down at the floor as he began to explain that night. He told Lisa and Bobby that they watched as the soul of a man floated up and into the room with them. It was like watching a puff of smoke in a breeze. The soul floated around the room as we watched it. It seemed to move around the room on the currents of air. The air from the air conditioner vent had pushed it toward the door, and just then, a nurse opened the door. The soul was sucked out into the hallway and disappeared in the light. What I didn't put in my journal was that we went there and watched several more people die, and each time their souls just floated on the air. Nathan went on to explain his theory about this. We have always assumed that ghosts couldn't leave the place where they were killed or died, being attached to the place of their death for eternity. I now believe that the soul is simply trapped inside the room or house, and only when the air movement is just right do they get to leave the room or house. Once outside, they can be gathered up by whatever is dragging them to the other side. This area needs more study too.

"What about walking on the other side? In one direction, things seem to be coming up quickly in the other direction, we seem to never get to them." Lisa asked.

Nathan began to explain why, when Lisa was on the other side and tried to walk further into the town she couldn't get anywhere. It's because over there the world is spinning slower than in this world, so walking over there is like walking on a treadmill. You must be able to move faster than the ground is spinning or move in the opposite direction than the ground's spin.

"That's why when you walk over there, the things in the distance seem to be coming at you, like a car coming toward you on the road. Lisa stated, confirming this information in her own head.

"Exactly right, you see it's not a matter of time over there, it's the spin of that world that creates the drive necessary to get anywhere. You only notice it when you're slowly walking toward something like whatever is in town. Nathan explained. He went on, the company is experimenting with things like roller skates, electric bikes and so on. They haven't been able to get them across as far as I know. Nathan was glad Lisa and Bobby had come and got him, and he wanted to put his knowledge to good use.

"I'll keep working on all of this. You guys stop Henry." Nathan spoke as he stood and went into the garage to start setting up his shop so he could help.

CHAPTER X

The Other Side of the Grave

Lisa sat back in her chair and realized she had notes on top of notes. She had notebooks, napkins, and even the back of a menu from a Chinese place. She wrote on anything she had when she needed to write something down. She knew she had to read through them all and try to figure out what all of this was. She walked around the house gathering up all the little notes she had. She started with the journal Tim had left her. Lisa reread it from cover to cover, only to realize there wasn't a whole lot in it. Tim had only scratched the surface when they crossed over, and he made a fatal mistake by taking from the other side. Lisa was going through the different notes she had and was trying to make a master list. She knew how the lens was created and why. She knew how to use the lens to find and follow a lost soul to the blue sphere of light and cross over, she even knew how to get back by waiting till another sphere opened, and she could push through it from the other side, coming back through. What she didn't know was all about the other side. She had so many questions about it, and she didn't really have the answers to any of those questions. Lisa went for a walk to try and get all this straight in her head, but after an hour or so, she was no closer to understanding what the other side was or how to try and use it from this side. She did know that figuring out how to use or control whatever was on the other side was the key to not only taking out Henry and his company but also to the success of the league.

MaryBeth had been working hard on trying to figure out some things too. She had come up with very little in the way of facts about the other side. She had, however, developed a good theory about why Hendersonville was the only place they could cross over. She explained it like this to Lisa. If you pull up the globe on the computer and center Hendersonville, it is not the center spot. It is close, though, MaryBeth explained. It must be that the portal connection is just there. It may line up from the other side to there, but that is the only explanation she has. Lisa smiled and nodded, though why it was in Hendersonville was now not as important to her as it once was.

Lisa sat at the kitchen table, staring at a stack of handwritten notes and questions she had collected. Suddenly, she had an idea. She would go over to the other side and try to figure this stuff out; over there, that's where the answers were. She would create a list of questions she needed answers to and see if she could answer those questions over there instead of trying to figure it out here in this world. She was going to put together a list of questions before she went over.

After looking through all her notes and questions, she decided on four questions. She wrote them down in order.

What is the other side? Why are the souls moving around like they are on missions? What about time? It seems to stop while over there. Finally, why is all the jewelry and stuff strewn everywhere? Lisa figured if she could get the answers to these questions, she would be better prepared to lead the league into helping humanity. She wrote the questions down on a notepad with a cover. One question per page, so she would have plenty of room to write her answer. Lisa decided she would go over by herself to look around. This was going to be a true fact-finding mission; no jewels would come back this time.

Lisa checked with Bobby and MaryBeth; she told them what she was going to do. Bobby wanted to go with her to watch her back, and as much as she wanted him there with her, she insisted he stay and keep working on the plan to take the company. MaryBeth told her she would go and help her figure things out, but again Lisa stood her ground and told MaryBeth to keep working on the take-down. Lisa planned to leave the next day and booked a plane ticket to Nashville. That evening, she was talking to Nathan and told him what she was doing. Nathan suggested she take a lens with a camera on it so she could take pictures, and they could analyze them after she returned. Lisa had read about being able to take pictures and videos with the lens, but none of her lenses could do that. Nathan had a lens with a built-in camera in his stuff. He dug it out and started charging it up. He suggested that Lisa put it on video and just leave it on while she was over there. Lisa also asked Nathan about a timer so she could track the amount of time she was there. He had a coach's digital timer that he used in some of his experiments; he gave it to Lisa. Lisa handed it back to him; she remembered how her digital watch had stopped while she was there. She would buy a stopwatch, old school, she thought as she smiled and walked confidently back into the house.

"We need you, Lisa, so please be very careful while you're in Hendersonville and on the other side." Nathan said as he put his hand on her shoulder. Lisa felt good about the people she had brought on to the team, and she appreciated the support they all were willing to give. The next morning, Bobby drove Lisa to the airport. He told her about a gun he had left in the mattresses of MaryBeth's house.

"You should take it with you when you head up to Hendersonville." He said with a stern look on his face.

We're in this thing now, so don't take any chances. Shoot first and figure it out later." He instructed. As Lisa sat there in the car listening to Bobby, the weight of the moment seemed to creep in on her. Lisa was concerned about going back to Hendersonville and about crossing over by herself; she had never done it by herself.

They made one stop on the way to the airport. A sporting goods store. Bobby followed Lisa, a bit confused, until she grabbed a stopwatch. They looked at each other and smiled as they climbed back into the car.

"Remember to shoot first and ask questions later, and don't take any stupid chances; be careful." Bobby instructed Lisa as she closed the door. Lisa just smiled and walked away. At her gate in the airport, she took her list out of her backpack and read it over one more time. The questions were solid, she thought, as she put them away and got in line to board the plane. On the plane to Nashville, Lisa was thinking hard about how she could find the answers to her questions. There was no one to ask, so she would have to figure it all out as she walked around on the other side. How long was she willing to stay on the other side? I should set a time limit. She thought as she sat down in her seat. The couple that sat beside her was on their way to upstate New York on vacation. The man who sat in the middle seat was very talkative and loud; Lisa was trying to ignore him so he wouldn't bother her all the way to Nashville. After the typical "Hi, how are you doing?" and "Where are you going?" questions. Lisa settled back and closed her eyes. As she sat there thinking about what she was doing, she found herself eavesdropping on the couple sitting next to her. The man ordered another drink, and his wife made a comment about not spending so much on this trip. The man told his wife they work too hard all year long to hold back on this trip. Then the man elbowed Lisa and laughed as he said, "Ya can't take it with you, right?" Lisa just smiled and nodded at him, closed her eyes and fell back into deep thoughts about the crossover she was about to do. Again, the weight of this crossing seemed to be heavier than all the crossings before. As Lisa was departing the plane, she was on high alert, looking for anyone who might be trying to get to her. Her head was on a swivel as she walked slowly through the airport toward the front door. As she walked through the terminal and looked around at all the people, she realized she would never be able to see if anyone was watching her here. She felt vulnerable and decided to get out of here as quickly as she could. She called up an Uber and headed for MaryBeth's house. MaryBeth had given her and Bobby a key just in case they ever needed it. Lisa went in and finally felt like she could relax. She sat quietly on the couch, just staring off into space, letting her mind unwind, from the almost panic she felt at the airport, she fell asleep. When she awoke, it took a second or two to realize where she was, and then it all came flooding back to her. She stood and stretched, then walked into the bedroom to get the gun Bobby had told her about. The gun was in a holster, so she strapped it onto her belt on her right side. She felt like a cowboy in a movie as she walked back into the living room to grab her backpack and head out. She wanted to grab a bite before crossing over, so she decided to stop at a diner in Millersville just outside of Hendersonville. As the driver headed out of Nashville toward Madison, Lisa was looking behind them closely. No one seemed to be following her, so she let herself relax a bit. In Millersville, she had the driver stop at a small restaurant on the side of the road to eat, sit quietly, and get prepared to cross over tonight. She watched the car drive away and turned to go into the diner. As she stood and waited for a table, she noticed a car pulling in, and she found herself staring at it. She watched as a man climbed out of the driver's side, followed by two little girls and his wife on the other side. Lisa smiled and shook her head, realizing no one knew she was here, as she was led back to a booth to sit in. The time was about seven thirty in the evening, and she would need to hang out here until it was time to go to the place on the back road. Lisa sat in the diner as long as she could and decided to go to the little church just down the road from where she would cross over. She stepped out on the sidewalk and was immediately grabbed by a man with a gun.

"Let's go." He said, pushing the barrel of the gun into Lisa's side. Lisa was startled by him and almost lost her balance as he pushed her toward his car. As Lisa was walking toward the car, she was wondering how she missed this asshole. Had he been following her the whole time? He took Lisa's arm and led her to the driver's side door of the car and shoved her in.

"Move it over." He instructed as he slid in behind Lisa. Lisa took the opportunity to pull the gun out and have it ready. The car was parked at the end of the parking lot and away from all the other cars. Lisa decided to take her chance now. She jerked the gun up from her side. She pointed the gun at the man's head and fired. His head snapped over to the left as the bullet passed up through his neck and out the other side. He grabbed his throat and was gurgling in his own blood as Lisa watched life run out of him in spurts. She opened her car door and left the man slumped in the car. As she was walking across the parking lot, she realized she still had the gun in her hand. She stopped and fumbled with it until she had it back in its holster. She took out her phone and, with trembling hands, ordered another Uber. Just a few minutes later, she was heading toward the little church where she would wait until it was time to cross over. At the church, she sat quietly in the shadows and waited. She kept a high level of awareness as she knew the company knew she was here. She was wondering how long that guy had been following her. Did they know she was at the airport? Did they discover she was here later? Then she remembered what the Uber driver had asked her on the way to Millersville.

"I feel like we have met before. Do you live around here?" The driver had asked.

"No." Was the only answer Lisa gave him. *He must've recognized me and called the company. That's why that asshole waited till I came out of the restaurant.* Lisa shook her head because she knew she wouldn't be able to sneak into Hendersonville much longer.

At about eleven o'clock, she started walking down the dark road toward the spot where she had waited many times before. She was looking and listening for anything that might be out of place. She had just killed one of the company guys, so they knew she was here.

She wondered how many people Henry had paid to work for and to watch for him. Maybe Henry had ties to someone at the airport, so when they saw my name, they alerted him. Lisa decided she couldn't worry about that right now as she was crossing over by herself for the first time. This time, she had quite a few reservations about the crossing. She was on her own, going over to a world she didn't really understand. In the past, when she had someone following her, she felt like she was in charge and knew exactly what she was doing. This time, she felt unsure for some reason. She reached the spot and stepped off the road into the shadows of the woods. She slowly took out the goggles and put them on. The goggles allowed her to raise her head and look through the lens or lower her head and look outside the lens. This allowed her to move faster and follow the lost soul easier. As Lisa stood there in the shadows of the woods, she let her mind go back to that first night with Tim. She remembered the smells, his smell. The rush of excitement from following him blindly. The absolute terror of going through the portal for the first time and the disbelief of what she saw on the other side. She heard the low rustle of wind in the trees and knew the time was near. Looking through the goggles, she saw the ragged-looking man being dragged across the road. Lisa fell in behind him and began to follow him. She had gotten good at following the souls and keeping up with them. When she saw the blue sphere in the distance, she hurried past the hole and pushed through to the other side.

Coming out into the decaying, foul-smelling world seemed to take all her thoughts away, and she couldn't remember any of the questions she needed to answer. As the soul came through the portal and started walking away from her, she took her backpack off and dug out her notes. Her eyes went to the third question she had written down about time. She looked at her watch; it had stopped at eleven-forty-two. She took the stopwatch out, started it, and put it in her pocket. She walked back the way she had come and onto the street of a town. As she stood there looking at the buildings through the lens and then not through the lens, it occurred to her that this was Hendersonville. It was not the main street, but the buildings and landscape looked familiar. She could see the souls moving around the streets like they each had their own mission, or were they just wandering around? What is this place? She thought, standing there looking around. Just then, in the corner of her eye, she caught another soul coming through a portal. The soul came through the portal and just started walking away. As the soul was walking, she noticed her ring had fallen off her hand and dropped to the ground. The necklace she was wearing came off and fell to the ground too.

"What the hell?" Lisa mumbled under her breath. She stood there trying to figure out what was happening when another soul came through a portal. All the jewelry dropped off this one too, as it walked away. The lost souls seemed unaware of the jewelry coming off as they walked purposefully away. Lisa noticed all the jewelry lying on the ground; it was everywhere.

"So, they come through, and any possessions they had in life fall away here." Lisa was still mumbling. Then she remembered what the guy on the plane had said: "You can't take it with you, right?" Lisa's mouth fell open as she came to the realization that this wasn't the other side of the grave; this was the grave. As she stood there, it all started making sense to her. She looked down at her notes and knew she had the answers to all her questions. This is the grave, and all souls must go through it to get to the next life, or world, or dimension, or whatever the hell it was. At the moment of death, the soul rises and is eventually brought here through the portals. They are here until they move on to the next world. The souls are moving around like they are on a mission because that's what they did in their life, and that's all they know for now. They must see the world they were in before they died. Their jewelry and all earthly possessions are left here in the grave, as they can't take anything with them to the next realm. As Lisa looked around at the decaying buildings and landmarks, it made even more sense. The smell was of decaying organic matter. The grave is always described as a box under the ground. There was no wind, no sun, and not even a breath of fresh air could enter here. The dim light is from the center of this place. There must be something over there, Lisa thought as she stood there. Lisa was looking through the lens at the buildings and streets because something wasn't right about what she was seeing. She was trying frantically to figure out what she was looking at when she remembered the camera in the lens. She started snapping pictures of the buildings and streets. It was while she was doing this that she realized the writing on the buildings and street signs was backwards. The doors and windows were on opposite sides. This is a reflection, she thought, standing there. The grave reflects the world you lived in, a reflection of every single person's life and memories. She watched a soul walk through a building she could see and disappear; this caused her to wonder how they could do that. Are the souls not real, or are they seeing the world and walking around in the world they left behind? So she is seeing and walking around in her world, even though she is not dead. Lisa looked at her list of questions again and realized she had the answers she needed. The rest of this could be figured out later. She tucked the list of questions away and headed for the edge of town to find a portal back across. As she stood there, looking for a portal to appear. She looked at the stopwatch; twenty-three minutes she had been on this side. This was longer than she had ever been on this side. As she closed her hand around the stopwatch and began looking for a portal again, she noticed a huge diamond ring laying right at her feet. She caught herself leaning down to pick it up. Just before she touched it, she stopped and jumped back, jerking herself back into the reality of where she was and what she was about to do. Lisa shook her head and strained to look through the goggles for a portal. The urge to pick up the ring at her feet was growing. She knew she had to get out of here now. Just then, a portal appeared, and she ran toward it. She ran through the blue sphere at full speed in a panicked state of mind.

Lisa came running and stumbled out of the portal on a small street; she was falling forward and was trying to keep her balance. She fell up against a sign and regained her balance. Stepping back, she read the sign, Portland Funeral Services. She gasped, realizing she was at a funeral home. The gasp turned to a smile and a small chuckle as she realized the irony of leaving the grave and ending up at a funeral home.

"At least I'm in the United States." She said as she smiled and looked around. She took out her stopwatch and stopped it. Twenty-four minutes was the time she had spent in the grave. She looked at her watch; eleven forty-two was the time still on her watch. She took out her phone, which by now had updated the time. Four fourteen in the morning was the time now. Lisa took out her notes and wrote all this down; she would figure it out later. She searched for her location and found, to her surprise, that she was in Portland, Australia. A wave of disappointment swept over her as she realized she was not in the United States after all. She felt exhausted and decided to find a hotel room first thing. She took off walking down the street, but soon found herself needing to sit down. She found a bench and took a seat, where she took out her phone and ordered an Uber to take her to a hotel. At the hotel, she could barely make it into the room. She felt like she had run a marathon; she was completely exhausted. She sent a text to MaryBeth saying I'm back, safe and in Australia., "I'm I'll be in touch tomorrow." Lisa dropped her phone onto the bed and fell into a deep sleep. When she awoke, she was disoriented and had no idea where she was or how long she had been asleep. She forced her eyes open and lifted her phone, seven-eighteen am. Lisa realized she had been asleep for more than twenty-seven hours. She slowly raised up and threw her legs over the side of the bed. After a few minutes, she stood and walked into the bathroom to shower. Lisa showered and put the same clothes she had been wearing back on. She gathered her stuff and headed down to check out. After checking out, she took a cab to the airport to fly back to Las Vegas. While she was waiting for her flight, she grabbed some food and sat quietly in the corner of the small restaurant, pondering what to do next. As she boarded the plane for the twenty-hour journey back to Vegas, she didn't have the mental energy to do anything but rest. Lisa sat and just stared out the window at the tarmac with planes slowly moving back and forth before and after takeoff. She sat there, going through the idea that she was going into her own grave when she crossed over. Suddenly, she had many more questions. Was there anything there that would give her an insight into her own fate? If so, would she even want to know? Lisa realized that when she was over there, Hendersonville was all she could see. What about the others, the followers she had taken over? Were they seeing their hometowns as graves? This was all really deep and would not help take down the company, she thought, shaking her head. On the plane, Lisa was trying very hard to put together a plan for the company. She finally gave up and decided to let Bobby handle the planning for that. She laid her head back and tried to sleep.

CHAPTER XI

Hostile Takeover

Bobby had made a list of the things they knew about the company. Things like Nathan, their guy who created the lens giving them the ability to cross over, now was on our side and in the garage working for us. They had killed Rick and were willing to kill anyone that gets in their way.

They are deeply embedded in at least the local police in Hendersonville. Lastly, we don't know the size of the company for sure or where Henry falls in the whole thing. We have found out where Henry is staying. Is he the leader, the main guy? Or is he just the guy in charge of this section? Bobby sat there staring at his list not really knowing where to begin.

"We have to go to Hendersonville." Lisa said picking up Bobby's notes to read them.

"That's where the fight is, and that's where were going to end this." Lisa finished speaking as she laid Bobby's notes back down. Lisa had been in bed for the last twelve hours or so after her long crossover, but now she was up and back in charge again.

The three of them packed their bags, leaving Nathan there where he would be safe. Rented a car and headed off to Hendersonville. During the drive, Lisa was going back over all the encounters she had with the company, and the one time she had spoken to Henry. The fact that Henry had his goons following her and thinking she would join him creeps her out. Henry thinks he's in complete control of every situation, that he has all the power, and that is where we can get him his own pride. Lisa started writing down ways to get Henry into the open. We could just keep on hijacking their crossers, until Henry shows himself. They could set a trap and bait Henry into coming out. Bobby looked over to see what Lisa was writing. Bobby took the pencil out of Lisa's hand and laid it down on her pad.

"This is a fight, and we will have to go after Henry and all his guys. Striking first and unannounced will give us our best chance." Bobby spoke with authority. Lisa just smiled at him and closed her notebook up. The rest of the trip was quiet, as each person was thinking of their part and how they could help with this.

In Nashville, they rented a room in two different hotels in case the company was watching MaryBeth's house. If they needed an exit strategy when they left the one in town, they wouldn't return. They would go to the other one that gave them easy access to the highway. Once they were all in the room, they each started doing their thing. Bobby left to go back to Hendersonville and get all the firepower he could manage to dig up. MaryBeth was busy searching for all the locations the company used in its operations. As Lisa sat quietly thinking about the other side and what was over there, she was startled by MaryBeth.

"Bingo!" MaryBeth said loudly.

"I have found the main headquarters for the company." MaryBeth was excited as she wrote down the address. She carried her laptop over to Lisa, and they scrolled through the information about the front company that the company was using to hide their real organization. It was an import company situated in a large warehouse on the outskirts of town. There were mainly open fields all around the compound with several fences blocking off sections of the property. There was only one way in and out of the complex. There were some trees on the ridge in front of the place where they could watch the place from. When Bobby got back, he had two duffel bags full of guns and ammo, and four old Army buddies with him.

They just wanted to shoot something it seemed, so they hit it off well with MaryBeth, who was always willing to shoot things. Lisa told Bobby what she and MaryBeth had found and handed him the address. Bobby wanted to go in tonight and poke around first. Then decide on when and how to take them down. Everyone agreed, and the rest of the afternoon was filled with quiet energy as they all prepared for the fight that was coming.

Bobby and his new crew headed off to see what they could find at the warehouse. MaryBeth was still searching through the internet to find any other information she could. Lisa was studying her notes; she believed the real answer to all of this was in actual crossing over and how the company had set itself up to be the one doing all the crossing. Wait, that was it, she thought. They are set up to do all the crossing over. If crossing over and collecting jewelry was the only things they were doing, they would have more money than they could hide at this point. Where was that money? Lisa thought as she let her mind go back to that diner when she met and talked to Henry. What was it, something on the other side that was making decisions about who dies and who lives here. Was the other side in control of this side, and Henry was just a puppet? These were all questions Lisa suddenly needed answers to, but didn't have. She sat back in her chair and closed her eyes. These answers would have to wait until after the takeover, Lisa thought as she sat rearranging the information in her head.

"Got the address." MaryBeth shouted, startling Lisa back into reality again. She wrote it out and laid it on the table so when Bobby got back, he would have it.

"The house Henry is staying in, Nathan sent it. He must've found it on Google Earth." Marybeth spoke as she went back to her computer. The night wore on as Lisa and MaryBeth were waiting for Bobby and his guys to get back.

Finally, around four in the morning, the door opened and in came Bobby. The noise jolted Lisa and MaryBeth awake. Lisa stood up and looked at Bobby, asking what he found with her eyes. Bobby just smiled and held up a handful of papers.

"I have the schedule Henry is using to crossover. It looks like it is based a lot on the moon phases. Although he has been going over on a half-moon and not waiting for the dark of the moon." Bobby finished speaking as MaryBeth took the papers out of his hand. She handed Bobby the address she had gotten from Nathan. Bobby read the words Henry's house and the address, and he just smiled.

"Do we want to attack now or wait for a crossing? Or maybe wait for several crossings?" Bobby asked as he checked the coffee maker for coffee. Bobby went on to explain the difference between the two tactics. If we wait for an opportune moment first, it may not come for a while. If we're waiting so we can get more money, we have plenty right now, and there will be more after we take over. If we go after Henry right now, tonight we have the element of surprise on our side, and we can take him out and take over before anyone even realizes we're in the building. He went on to explain his plan to Lisa and MaryBeth. We go to this house on the river, Bobby was holding up the scrap of paper MaryBeth had written on we take Henry out, and anyone we think is loyal to him. Then we go to the main building, march in and proclaim our victory. We start calling the shots with all of Henry's contacts, including the police. By this time tomorrow morning, we will own this whole damn thing. Lisa was impressed by Bobby's willingness to just plow through the doors and take over, but she also knew it wasn't going to be that easy. Lisa had been working through this plan for days now. She started explaining what she thought about Bobby's plan. She went into it. "First of all, getting to Henry is going to require more than just kicking in the door. You don't know what, who or how many are behind that door. Let's just say he has enough guys there to take you out. Then he knows about us, and we are all going to have to run for our lives. But, even if you do get Henry and his men, the others involved with the banks and businesses aren't just going to sign everything over and let us have it. Then let's talk about the

Hendersonville police department. Those guys and gals have done some pretty sketchy things, not something any of them want out in the open. So, what are we going to do, kill a bunch of cops, or maybe talk them into coming over to our side? I'm not sure what to do, but charging ahead without a plan is a bad idea." Bobby just nodded in agreement and sat down with a reheated cup of coffee. Lisa continued, "I've been writing down notes and lists for a long time, and I think I have an idea of what we need to do. Henry needs to disappear but still be alive in case we need him or his signature, or even his fingerprint. Once we have him detained, then and only then can we approach the police. They must trust that we will not only continue to pay them but also make it even more lucrative for them. They have to trust us enough to join us. The businesses and banks will be easier. We just need to use Henry's signature to add one of us to the open accounts and contracts, then we have control. Then and only then can we take over the operation and yes, get rid of Henry." Lisa sat back as she finished talking.

"So, if we kidnap Henry and then contact his people. What do you think they will do, fight or join us?" MaryBeth asked from behind her monitor.

"Not sure. There are a lot of variables to this whole thing." Lisa responded, looking over her notes. Bobby stood up and said, "They'll fight," as he left the room and went to get some sleep. MaryBeth left and went to the grocery store for food, and Lisa sat down to form the plan. Lisa wrote out what she thought would work best to take the company down. Stake out Henry's house to decide when we can grab him. Take something of his to show the workers in the company shop. We have him, and we are in control. Find evidence of police involvement and corruption. Contact the police chief and tell him we have the evidence and explain our ultimate plans for doing good things with the money. Allow him to do the right thing and help us turn this into a good thing. If they refuse? She wasn't sure about that last question. Let MaryBeth figure out the books and money flow and get ourselves moving in the right direction.

Later that day, Bobby and his four guys went to the house where Henry was staying. They set up and watched the house for Henry's movements. For three days, they watched the house and saw several people coming and going, including the police chief and three of his lieutenants. Each one of those days, Henry left the house at two o'clock and went to the company headquarters. He stayed there until six o'clock. He left there and went to a small restaurant to eat, and was home by eight o'clock each of those days. When he returned, the car that was driving him left him there by himself. That's when we should hit him, Bobby thought. Bobby called Lisa and told her they were ready to move on Henry, and how they were going to do it. Lisa agreed, and her and MaryBeth armed themselves and got ready to move. The next day, after Henry left to go to the company headquarters, Bobby's team moved up to the house. They could see four men sitting around a table, eating and drinking. Bobby kicked in the door, and they rushed the four men. Everything paused for an instant as all the men stared at each other. One of Henry's men tried to get his gun out and was shot instantly. The others slowly raised their hands. Suddenly, one of the men with Bobby just shot them in the head and stood there smiling. With the four men dead, they dragged their bodies into a bedroom and left them there. Now they waited.

At the same time, MaryBeth had been going through the financial documents Nathan had given her, along with the ones she found online. It took a while, but she figured out the initials of the people receiving payments. She found the police chief's initials, along with those of everyone who had received money from the company. There was one set of initials that didn't match anyone's name though. They were written off to the side, not part of the main list. MaryBeth figured it was an attorney or someone who may have found out more than they wanted to. She just figured they were probably already dead, skipped it and moved on.

At the house, Bobby had put each of his team in specific spots to cover all the angles when Henry returned. Just after eight o'clock the car pulled up to let Henry out. Henry got out, but was not alone he had three men with him. As Henry and the three men entered, Bobby heard them talking about Nathan, and Lisa. Henry told the other men he wanted them dead as soon as they could get it done. Henry stopped short as soon as he saw Bobby standing there, pointing a gun at him. The other three men froze as well. Bobby pulled Henry roughly by the collar over to one side. As soon as he had Henry clear, his men opened fire on the three men left standing in the kitchen. They all fell limply in a pile as they died. Bobby turned Henry around and put handcuffs on him.

"You belong to us now, asshole. Let's go." Bobby said matter-of-factly. One of Bobby's men had already left to get the car and was pulling up as Bobby, Henry, and the other three men came out of the house. They took Henry to an abandoned barn Bobby knew about and locked him in a small room. Bobby told one of his guys to stay there and if that door opens or anyone shows up other than me, kill them. Bobby called Lisa and told her they had Henry, and he was locked away. Bobby told Lisa he and the other three were going back to Henry's house to search for more information.

In their search, they found several folders with pages of notes, calendars, and tally sheets. There was also a folder with lists of bank accounts, stock market numbers, and businesses the company had been working with. Then he found the police file with all the bad cops' names and what they had done. There was another file with just two letters on it, maybe initials, Bobby thought as he stacked everything up. Bobby shoved all this information into a briefcase, and they all headed for the door. Two of his guys stepped out on the porch only to be shot and killed. The other man jumped back and shoved Bobby back inside. He pointed to the side window, and Bobby headed toward it. When Bobby reached the window and started to climb out, his buddy stepped out onto the porch and started shooting at Henry's men. This allowed Bobby to run up the bank and onto the road. Bobby never looked back at the house, but when the shooting stopped, he knew his friends were gone. He hoped that his guy had taken out Henry's men. It took Bobby a couple of hours to get far enough away from the house to feel safe, pause and catch his breath. He collected himself and ordered an Uber, then headed to the hotel.

Once back at the hotel Bobby told Lisa and MaryBeth what had happened. He went on to explain that Henry was locked in a room in a barn where nobody would find him. Bobby knew if any of Henry's men had survived, they would already be back at the warehouse, and their element of surprise would be gone.

"We should go now." Bobby insisted.

Lisa grabbed her go bag and one of Bobby's guns. MaryBeth grabbed both of her guns and shoved them into their holsters. The three of them headed for the company warehouse. The warehouse was a buzz with commotion. People were coming and going, and they all looked worried. One of the garage doors was open, so they decided to sneak in there. Once inside, they all three headed to the office. There were five men in the office, two of them were on the phone and seemed to be quite upset and yelling. Bobby knew at least one of Henry's men had gotten back to the others, so total surprise was not an option now. Bobby eased the door open and slid in, pointing his gun as the five men realized he was in there. Lisa and MaryBeth followed him in with their guns pointed too.

"Just listen." Lisa said, looking at the one she thought was in charge.

"We have Henry, and we are taking control of the company." Lisa said, waving her gun back and forth.

"You can either join us, and we all get to carry on, or not." Lisa said, putting her gun up to one of the men's heads.

"Who is in charge, now that Henry is not here?" Bobby asked, moving his eyes back and forth from man to man.

Four of the men looked at one of the men who still had the phone up to his ear. The man slowly hung the phone up and dropped it on the desk. He nodded in agreement and just stared at Bobby.

"No one else needs to die. Just listen to us." Bobby said, staring back at the man.

Suddenly, a gunshot rang out, and the office window shattered. The five men started trying to get their guns out, but MaryBeth was quicker. She fired five times, and all the men fell dead. Bobby turned his attention to whoever shot the window out. A quick pop of his gun, and that guy went down. The last of Henry's men came at them all at once six men hiding behind whatever they could and firing as they moved up. Lisa and MaryBeth dropped down and was shooting from the ground, Bobby started shooting from where he was. After several minutes of weaving and bobbing Henry's men were down and either dead or wounded. MaryBeth jumped up and ran out of the office, shooting as she went. She took care of the wounded men, killing them all. Bobby just looked at MaryBeth and shook his head, puzzled by her willingness to kill. Lisa was looking all around the warehouse for other men. Bobby had run out the door to the outside, looking around.

"Clear!" Bobby said as he came back in.

"Was that it? That's the company?" Lisa asked, looking through some papers on the desk. They all smiled at one another, but they knew they were going to have to face the police too, and they wouldn't be able to just shoot everyone there. Lisa didn't know what she was looking for, but she couldn't stop rifling through the papers on the desk. She didn't even know if this was Henry's desk. The silence seemed overwhelming as all three relaxed their minds just a bit as they figured out their next steps. MaryBeth had just reloaded her gun and put it back in its holster. Suddenly, all the exterior doors burst open, and they were surrounded by twenty or more cops. "Well, now we know how many cops are on the company's payroll." Bobby said as he stood there with his hands up.

"Bobby Riley." The police chief shouted as he walked into the room. Bobby noticed MaryBeth looking like she was going to pull her gun. Bobby cleared his throat to get her attention and shook his head. MaryBeth took his advice and relaxed. All three of them had their hands raised up above their heads. The police chief motioned for them to put them down as he stepped up in front of Lisa.

"I believe you must be Lisa Riley." The chief said, half-smiling. "Henry was right about you; you are quite the beauty. What do you think is going to happen now?" the chief stared at MaryBeth as he finished talking.

Lisa summoned all her courage and cleared her mind so she could speak to the police chief.

"We have Henry, you'll never find him, and we will deal with him. We would like to offer you the same deal he was giving you, maybe even more. But we want to take the money and do good with it." Lisa stared as hatefully as she could at the chief as she talked.

The chief was laughing as he started talking "What makes you think I have a deal with this Henry person you speak of. Maybe I don't even know who that is. Maybe, we just kill all of you, and we take over this enterprise for good." The chief was looking sideways at Lisa as he finished.

"We have an internet trail a mile long with you and all of your men being named and described by what you have done and what you have taken from the company." MaryBeth asserted.

She now had the police chief's attention. MaryBeth went on. I have it all in a file and saved set to send, and if I don't come back and turn the countdown timer off, it all goes to the federal government. Several agencies from the government will be knocking on your door and crawling up your ass in the next day or two. Then you can explain all of this to the feds. There was a long pause in that room as the police chief pondered what his next move would be. After what seemed several minutes, he turned to Bobby, smiled and nodded.

"Well, it would seem that y'all have this here company under control. So, I don't think me, or my men need to be here." The police chief spun his finger up in the air, and all of the police turned to leave as he spoke. The chief turned as he was walking out to speak to Lisa.

"I will be expecting a visit from you, Mrs. Riley, in the next few days so we can negotiate our new terms and figure out how we can help you. With this new business venture, you are undertaking." When the police chief finished talking, he slowly walked out of the warehouse, and all the police officers left.

Bobby breathed a sigh of relief and smiled at Lisa. Lisa was calculating her next move with the police already and didn't notice Bobby.

"That was a great idea, MaryBeth, taking all that information and putting it in a file with a countdown on it." Bobby said.

"Huh, what file?" MaryBeth said as she started checking the dead men for things. She looked up and just smiled at Bobby. Bobby knew he was working with a couple of sharp ladies. When MaryBeth finished taking the dead men's stuff, she went and got one of the company's laptop computers. She sat it on the dead man's chest and raised his head up for facial recognition. She went to three of the corpses, and on the fourth one, the computer opened. MaryBeth immediately changed the login and password, then she began going through all the company's stuff. Lisa sat down in one of the office chairs and looked at Bobby. Marybeth took her phone out and sent a text to Nathan, saying they had taken control of the company and would be in touch tomorrow.

"Let's take Henry to the other side." Lisa said. "I've got an idea." Bobby just smiled and nodded. The three of them decided to stay there for the night and get a fresh start tomorrow morning. Lisa and Bobby found a place to stretch out, but MaryBeth was too engrossed in the company's files and information to stop and sleep. The next morning, when Lisa woke up and looked around, she saw Bobby still asleep on an old couch. MaryBeth was asleep with her head down on the desk where they left her the night before. Lisa stood and stretched. It had been a while since she had slept in a chair. She started looking for a coffee maker and some coffee. A few minutes later, Bobby awoke and stood up stretching as well.

"I need to get rid of all these bodies first thing today." Bobby said, looking around at the men still laying where they had fallen. Lisa nodded as she turned on the coffee maker.

"I'm starving. I'm going to make a breakfast run." MaryBeth said, leaning back in her office chair. She stood up to leave but stopped at the door, looked back, and smiled, then headed out for breakfast. Lisa, meanwhile, was figuring out how she could use Henry on the other side to see what was over there and if she could control it. We have to be able to follow one of the lost souls all the way into town when we cross over. She thought as she sat down at one of the desks. Bobby left to go check on his guy, who was watching Henry and take him some supplies. Lisa watched him go and then set about figuring out how to move in the opposite direction in the other world. She remembered what Nathan had said about them trying to take skates and other things across, but they couldn't. Why, she wondered, she had taken carry-on bags across and her backpack. She picked up her phone and called Nathan. When Nathan answered, she asked about taking skates or skateboards through the portal. Nathan wasn't really sure, but he remembered hearing the crossers talking one evening about not wanting to be the person to get across with the skates, because they would be expected to go and see what the hell is over there. So maybe it's not that they couldn't, it's that they wouldn't take them across. Henry would believe them if they told him they couldn't; he was all about the money anyway. When Nathan finished, Lisa knew what she had to do. She wondered what the best thing for traveling over there would be. She headed into the back part of the warehouse, where she found several electric bikes they are too heavy to drag through the woods, she thought. Roller skates, skateboards and those electric things that you lean into to ride. She decided it would have to be a skateboard. They were light easy to carry, and could go at whatever speed they needed. She grabbed three of them and went back up front. In the office, MaryBeth had returned with several bags of fast-food breakfast, and they began to eat. Bobby came in shortly after with the guy he had left watching Henry.

"Where's Henry?" Lisa almost shouted.

"He's right here." Bobby said, leading him along with a bag over his head. "I needed help moving these bodies, and all the other guys are dead. So here we are. There's a cage in the back, I'm going to put him in there." Bobby just walked by as he spoke. Lisa, Bobby and Bobby's friend worked the rest of the day disposing of the bodies of all the dead men. They stacked them all in a cargo trailer sitting in the back of a vacant piece of the property. As darkness fell, Bobby and his guy went back to Henry's house to get those bodies. They were all gone though, Bobby saw an unmarked police car sitting down the street, and he figured the police had taken this place. Later that evening, Lisa shared her plan for taking Henry to the grave. Bobby, you and I can take Henry and those skateboards across we'll use the skateboards to follow one of the lost souls till we find whatever it is over there. Then we'll use Henry to see what the hell it is. Bobby liked the plan but knew Henry wasn't going to go along quietly. So, they would have to be ready at all times to just shoot him.

The next night, around eleven o'clock Lisa, Bobby, and one handcuffed Henry climbed out of the car in the same spot on the road where this all began for Lisa. Bobby and Lisa had their guns out and pointed at Henry. Lisa had shared her plan with Henry, but he didn't have anything to say, he just sat and smiled at her. It was almost like he knew something she didn't. Lisa had MaryBeth go through as much of the company's information as she could about the other side. She found very little information which told Lisa either that Henry didn't know or that he was really keeping that part of this hidden. Either way, Lisa knew she wasn't prepared for this but there was no better time or way to try and figure it out.

Lisa took a deep breath as she heard the low rustle of the wind in the trees like before.

"Get ready." She said, looking at Henry.

"There, there it is." Bobby said, looking through the viewer. He grabbed Henry and started walking fast. Lisa grabbed the skateboards they had tied together and reached around to check her backpack. As they made their way through the woods, it wasn't long till they could see the dim blue portal up ahead and sped up past the lost soul. Lisa went through with the skateboards, and Bobby pulled Henry through right behind her. Once on the other side, they started untying the skateboards and running to keep up with the lost soul, now walking like a young man. Henry fell down with his hands cuffed behind him. Bobby grabbed him up and took the cuffs off. He put his gun right in Henry's face and smiled. They ran for a short time, then came to a road where they jumped on their skateboards. Henry wasn't fighting or trying to hold them up. It was like he wanted to go and see what was there too. The three of them skated right past the lost soul and were making progress toward the light way in the distance. As they kept going, they began to see more and more of the lost souls just wandering about, aimlessly. Most of them were walking alone, but there were some walking together, and even one group with four souls in it. Lisa wondered about this for the first time.

"Why are some of the souls alone and some together?" Lisa asked as they were skating along on the road. Bobby started noticing the pairings too, but wasn't giving it too much thought as he was focused on Henry and what they were doing.

"It's who you die with." Henry said.

"If you die alone, as most people do, then you are in here alone, but if you die with others, you are in here with them, maybe forever." Henry looked at Lisa as he spoke with a smug smile, which Lisa just wanted to slap off his stupid face. Suddenly, they were close enough to see a building with light pouring out of the windows and doors, so bright they could barely stand to look at it. The light made Lisa feel like she was leaving a dark movie theater and walking directly into the sunlight, it was more light than her eyes could take in. There was heat too, Lisa could feel it on her face and arms. She leaned her head back to look through the lens at the house. The light was red in the viewer, and the lost souls that had just come over were walking into it, and into the building. Some would come back out and wander around, while others would not come back out. The three of them just stood there looking at this house of light. Lisa was snapped back into reality by Henry's laugh. When she looked at him, he was almost trance-like, never taking his eyes off the house.

"Ok, time to answer all your questions Henry." Lisa said, yanking him up to her. Henry looked at her and smiled like he had just won something.

"Look, I'll go in there and see, but you will see me again, and I will take your soul." Henry said, smiling. Lisa looked to Bobby for an answer, Bobby nodded.

"Keep your gun pointed at his head." Bobby told Lisa as he turned Henry around and shoved him forward. Henry looked at both of them and smiled with an evil look, then started walking slowly toward the building and its light energy. As he got to the doorway, he had his hands up to block what he could from the light energy. Then he simply disappeared into the light. There was a long silence, then a sound like a high wind blowing, and the flow of lost souls into the building stopped for a few seconds. The light energy brightened then dimmed, and that was followed by the scream of a dying man. The lost souls resumed their walking into the building. Lisa looked at Bobby, she just turned and started walking the other way.

"We need more information, maybe Nathan can come over and figure it out." Lisa said, looking back at Bobby, who had started walking also.

Inside the house, Henry had put one of his hands up over his eyes because his eyelids couldn't keep the light out. He was feeling his way through the lighthouse with the other hand. Henry found a wall, and he began to follow it. The wall gave way to a doorway through which Henry stuck his head through. There was a force that was trying to pull Henry into this world. When Henry opened his eyes, he could see vast barren lands and a red sun. He pulled back on the wall with all his might. He had to use both hands, the force he was pulling back was everything he had, to the point of screaming at the top of his lungs. He made it back into the house. His eyes were beginning to adjust to the light just enough for Henry to make out the other doorways. Henry realized in that moment if he could find the doorway back to his world, maybe he could find them and kill them all. Being alive meant that Henry could resist the force of being pulled into a random world until he found his old world. As Henry went through the light house, sticking his head in each doorway to see where it went. He saw worlds that were on fire, underwater, filled with thick smoke, cities in ruins. Henry began to feel himself changing physically, and he knew he wouldn't last much longer in this place. The pain of his twisting flesh and bending bones was almost too much to stand, and he was about to collapse when he found it. Henry saw the cities and blue sky of his old world, so he let go and was pulled into it. When the light, heat, and pressure stopped, Henry found himself lying in tall grass, writhing in pain.

It only took a minute or so for Lisa and Bobby to walk the other way and get back to the woods where they could find a portal. It was almost routine for Lisa now as she stood there watching through her glasses till she saw a portal that was close enough. She pointed, and she and Bobby crossed back over to their side of the grave. They came out in what seemed like a garden that had been harvested. Lisa instinctively hunkered down; Bobby followed. Lisa pulled out her phone and searched for their location.

"Crawford, Nebraska, well, at least we're in the United States." Lisa said with a smile. She pointed due west, and they started walking toward Crawford. Once they were on a road, Lisa texted her pilot and asked to be picked up. A few minutes later, the pilot texted back Lusk, Nebraska airport, six hours. Lisa ordered an uber and they were off to Lusk. They didn't realize until they were in the airport that a whole day had passed here while they were over there. Lisa knew time went faster here and seemed to stop there, but this was the first time she really felt it. Did time move faster because they were near the center of town, or maybe because they traveled further against the spin. How far had they traveled anyway? They took a seat on the little plane and waited to get back to Hendersonville. Lisa was so very tired, and by the looks of Bobby, he was too. Spending too much time in the grave seemed to take the life energy from them, Lisa thought as she closed her eyes.

Once back in Hendersonville, they headed straight to the warehouse. MaryBeth was there, and Nathan had flown in too. They had a theory about what the building with the light energy was. It sent souls to other dimensions, but once there, they had no idea what would happen to them. Lisa was now turning her attention to the police chief and what he would want out of all of this. She called the chief and asked him to come over and put a deal together. MaryBeth had actually put all the files and information into a computer file. She had all the hard copies stacked up neatly on her desk, with each of the dirty cops' names on their file; she wanted them to know she had the dirt on them. The police chief showed up with all his dirty cops by his side. They all walked in and stood around the chief. The chief smiled and began.

"I will be taking charge of all of this, and my department will be running the crossings from now on. You all can stay on and work for me as long as you do what I say." The police chief spoke as if he had no worries at all. Lisa heard the low rustle of the wind in the trees and grabbed her glasses. Coming through the door was a being, but it wasn't moving like the other lost souls. It moved in spurts so fast that Lisa couldn't see it until it stopped in front of the police chief. It opened its mouth, and the chief's soul left his body and was being dragged off silently, screaming and writhing by some unknown force. The being then opened its mouth and swung its head around toward all the remaining police officers. Their souls left their bodies in the same way, and they all fell dead on the floor. The being turned toward Lisa, and Lisa could see that it was Henry. No, it was some twisted form of Henry, he was barely recognizable, but it was Henry. His flesh was moving in knots up and down his arms, his bones were bending in places they should not be bending. Henry stared at Lisa, and she knew he had made it through the lighthouse and back into this world. But at what cost Lisa was looking at a monster. Henry snapped back and threw his arms out in an uncontrollable fit of pain. Then, looking straight at Lisa, he began to open his mouth. Bobby pulled out his pistol and fired six shots into the creature, but they passed right through, and Henry turned his attention to Bobby. They all just stood there in disbelief, looking at this creature that had come out of its own grave. Nathan had been fumbling around in a bag he had, and he suddenly pulled out an old flashlight and turned it on. There was a blue light energy beam that came out. Lisa realized he had put on the goggles and was seeing Henry too. Nathan pointed the flashlight at Henry, and he winched in pain. Henry turned toward Nathan and began to open his mouth. Nathan started walking toward Henry, keeping the light beam on his chest. The light was hurting Henry, and he was swinging his arms to try to stop the light. Henry began to seem weak, and he fell to one knee, then both knees and then back onto his back. He laid there, writhing until his soul rose up, still fighting the blue light energy beam. Suddenly, his soul stopped fighting, seemed to go limp and was being dragged off by some unknown force. Henry's twisted body lay there in its ragged clothes on the floor. Nathan turned the old flashlight off and just stood there, his hands shaking as he looked around the room at the league.

"What the hell was that?" Bobby said, walking over to where Henry's body was lying.

"I'm not sure what I'm going to call it, but I'm glad I brought it." Nathan said.

Lisa was stunned by everything that had just happened, and she knew they had a lot of figuring things out to do. Bobby and his friend started carrying all the bodies out and loading them into a truck. Turns out there was a big hole the company had dug in its plan to get rid of bodies way back on the property behind the warehouse. MaryBeth was going through all the dead men's clothes and pockets. Collecting whatever she could. Lisa decided they should all pack up everything they could, and after they get rid of all these bodies, they retreat to someplace where they could work all this out. By the end of the day, they were all on the road back to Vegas. They left Bobby's friend there to watch and keep up with the warehouse until they returned.

CHAPTER XII

Enter the World Stage

Back in Vegas they all unpacked their gear and stuff they had brought from the warehouse. Bobby was curious about the strange blue ray Nathan had taken Henry out with. He wanted answers about it, almost demanding them. Nathan pulled out the flashlight and turned it on, allowing the pale blue light to flow from the handle. He suddenly turned on the light and pointed it straight at Bobby. Bobby dropped to the floor like he had been shot while getting out of the blue light's path. Nathan turned the light toward himself and chuckled at Bobby on the floor. It does nothing to us on this side. It destroys, controls or does something to the souls from the other side. I haven't crossed with it yet to see what it would do to one of us over there in the other world. Nathan went on to explain how when our light energy is pushed through a certain lens and passed through a certain gaseous mixture, it comes out in the high-intensity beam. That's all he knew right now, but was going to study it and figure it all out.

"How did you know it would work on the lost souls?" Bobby asked as he got up from the floor.

"We tested it on one of them outside of Hendersonville." MaryBeth said as she was hooking up her computers.

"Me and Nathan drove out there and waited till a soul came by. Instead of following it, we used his blue light thingy on it. That sucker just went crazy like it was being killed again, then gave in and was dragged off to the grave." MaryBeth chuckled.

"So, you didn't really know what would happen if you used it on Henry." Bobby said.

"Well, I had a good idea, and it was better than anything you had at the time." Nathan said as he recapped the light and laid it on the desk. Bobby picked it up, turned it on and off, and studied it like a new piece of equipment. MaryBeth had started searching for more ways to handle the money. Nathan was pouring over some equations he had written down. Lisa looked around the room and decided they needed to come up with some objectives and some plans to meet those objectives, or they would be doing just what interested them at the moment and not really accomplishing what this discovery could accomplish for the planet.

Lisa set about cleaning the whiteboard she had bought earlier, setting it up and pulling everyone together. She started by asking each person what they wanted the league to accomplish.

Everyone agreed they wanted to use the money to help the people of Earth, and to help the Earth itself heal from all the pollution and misuse of the land. This was a great and noble objective. The problem was that no one knew exactly how to do this in the most effective way. They decided to start with the money. Henry had not only put millions of dollars into online entities, businesses, the stock market and a host of other ventures. He had also stored vast sums in boxes in the back of the warehouse, and who knows where else. MaryBeth was going to track down all the online money to find a total and move the money into a working account for them to have at their disposal. Bobby and Nathan were going back to Hendersonville. Nathan's lab was there, and Bobby could work on counting the money stored there. Lisa was going to focus on the crossings and figure out all she could about them and the other side. As Lisa and MaryBeth watched Bobby and Nathan pack up all their things to go back to Hendersonville for good, they decided they would go back too. No reason not to at this point.

Three days later, they arrived in Hendersonville and moved everything they had into the warehouse. Lisa went to Henry's Lake house, cleaned up all the blood splatter, threw out the bloody rugs and moved into it. MaryBeth gave up her rental house in Nashville and found a rental there in Hendersonville. Bobby went back to his house in Hendersonville. It had been ransacked, but nothing was gone, so he put it back together and settled in there. Nathan went back and forth between Lisa's place and Bobby's place, but mostly stayed at the warehouse working. Three weeks flew by before they knew it, and they came together on a Friday evening to list everything they had accomplished.

MaryBeth had found and secured thirty-eight million dollars online. Most of the money was still growing in the stock market and other money accounts. She was able to take ownership of the funds by using Henry's passwords, which she had found, and his electronic signature. Bobby had counted all the money stashed in the back, a little more than nineteen million dollars, sitting in boxes in the back. Nathan was still working on the lenses and what we could do with them. Lisa had calculated that other than the money on the other side, there wasn't anything they could control or use to control things in this world, at least right now. She had asked Nathan to work on building a lens that could be worn to look into the light energy coming out of the building on the other side. She had also decided to try using different methods of collecting the jewelry using different tools, or gloves. She was wondering if it was touching the jewelry with the flesh of a follower and taking it from the grave, or if it was truly the act of taking it from the grave. So that it didn't matter what they used, maybe it wasn't about gathering the stuff up at all, it was simply who carried it back across. If she could figure that out, she could create specialized teams of grave robbers to cross over and bring back the stash.

Nathan was trying to develop the blue energy light ray he had discovered into a renewable energy source. He was making progress in this area, but it was slow going by himself.

Lisa decided to maximize the positive impact of millions of dollars on the Earth, they would need to focus on the sustainable development of renewable energy and environmental conservation. They could support education and research in both areas of study. Investing in projects that address climate change, such as renewable energy and infrastructure. She was going to investigate initiatives that promote sustainable agriculture and protect natural ecosystems. Bobby suggested investing in our schools and funding educational programs focused on environmental awareness and scientific research for long-term solutions.

Lisa was happy they had defeated the company and were moving forward with using the money for good. She did, however, already miss the thrill of crossing over and decided to make a crossover to see what else she could figure out. She needed to figure out if it was touching the jewelry that caused the followers to be dragged back, or whether it was taking the jewelry without touching it, but carrying it back across. She would talk a couple of people into following her over and try some sort of grabber for one, and the other would not touch the stuff and just carry the bags back through. If either one survived, she would have her answer. Lisa shared her plan with the league and left the next day to go back to Sarasota and find a couple of people.

In Sarasota, Lisa was glad her house was still there, and although it had been ransacked and trashed by the company, it was still in good shape. She spent more than a week cleaning it up and organizing it. She was sitting on her patio enjoying the evening air when her neighbors, Nick and Debbie from two houses down, knocked on the patio door.

"Come in." Lisa said, getting up to open the door. The couple came in, and they spent the next several hours catching up and finishing a second bottle of wine. Lisa hadn't been so relaxed in a while and felt really good when she crawled into bed. The next morning, feeling a bit hungover, she remembered she had made breakfast plans with Nick and Debbie and set about getting ready.

She met them at a breakfast place and, after a few minutes, decided they could be the ones to follow her over to try her experiment. She spent the next couple of days with Debbie shopping and just hanging out. She mentioned the prospect of crossing over without the details to Debbie to get her reaction. Debbie said she and Nick needed some adventure, and if they could make some money in the process, that would be even better. They decided to talk to Nick that night at Lisa's house, she would make dinner for them. Lisa called MaryBeth and told her what she was doing. She asked Nathan to buy a pair of gloves he thought would work and the best grabber he could find, along with a couple of flexible carry-on bags. Over dinner, she caught Nick up on the idea and shared more of the details with both. Nick only needed to put in a two-week notice for a vacation of a week off, and they would be good to go. During those two weeks, Lisa realized Nick was very overbearing to Debbie. She also realized Debbie's knowledge of social media and working for charitable organizations and environmental causes would make her a great person to have on her team. Lisa approached Debbie with a different idea. She would take Nick and one of his buddies across to try the experiment. Leaving Debbie to join the league. Debbie asked Nick to get one of his buddies to go over instead of her, and he was surprisingly willing to do it. Nick got it all set up with his buddy Jamie, and they were all good to go. Once Lisa heard they were in, she booked the private jet to take them to Hendersonville. The four of them stayed in Lisa's Lake house that night, Lisa planned to take them to the warehouse the next morning. She checked with MaryBeth to see if they had got all the things she needed. MaryBeth said they had it all.

The next morning, bright and early, the four of them headed off to the warehouse. There she introduced them, MaryBeth, Bobby and Nathan. Nathan showed them the grabber, and the gloves. He told them they would have nothing to worry about, he had tested them both. Nick was curious about why they needed the grabber and gloves, and Nathan explained that the stuff on that side was contaminated with the putrid semi-dead molecules, and they had seen some damage to other followers' hands. This was only to protect them from any harmful side effects. Lisa spoke up and declared that they would only use the gloves on this trip. Nick was obviously shaken by this and pulled Debbie off to the side. They began to argue, and Nick grabbed Debbie and raised his hand like he was going to hit her.

"I wouldn't do that if I were you." Bobby called out from his desk. Nick just stormed off outside, and Jamie followed. Lisa went to Debbie and hugged her. Debbie looked at Lisa through her tears and mouthed the words "I'm sorry." Lisa took Debbie into her office and sat her down. She told her to just relax, she and the league would take care of her. The rest of the day was uneventful as the league went on with its business and Lisa prepared to crossover.

That night Lisa, Nick and Jamie were driven by Bobby's friend out of the secluded back road to cross over. They stood there waiting at the side of the road for several minutes. While they waited, Lisa explained how this was going to work.

"Nick, you will wear the gloves and gather the jewelry up to fill the bags with. You must not touch any of it with your bare hands." Lisa was being as serious as she could. She then turned to Jamie.

"Jamie, you will only carry the bags over and back you will not touch any of the jewelry. Once Nick puts on the gloves, he can't take them off until we are back over here. Lisa looked at both men as she finished, and they nodded. Lisa turned her attention back to the lens in her goggles and tried to find a soul to follow. She heard the low rustle of the wind in the trees. The lost soul came up behind them and almost passed right through them.

"Come on." Lisa said as she started following the soul.

"Keep up with me and don't hesitate when we get to the portal." Lisa was talking as she was walking behind the lost soul. They followed the lost soul for a long while and were deep in the woods when Lisa saw the pale blue light up ahead. She picked up her pace to pass the lost soul. Nick and Jamie were right behind her. When they reached the portal, Lisa pushed Nick through and grabbed Jamie's arm, pulling him through just before the lost soul. On the other side, Lisa saw the total fear and astonishment on their faces. She pushed Nick in the direction they needed to go, and Jamie fell in behind them, carrying the bags. As they came out of the woods and started down the decaying street, Lisa wasn't in as much of a hurry as she used to be.

"Jamie, do not touch any of the jewelry." Lisa reminded him as they approached an old building. Lisa went up to the door and kicked it in. The trio walked into the building.

"Fill up your bags! But do not touch the stuff with your hands!" Lisa commanded Nick as she set up to watch the street. She watched two of the souls come down the street and go into the woods, where they just disappeared. She stood there, wondering what this was all about. Where were they going? Lisa turned her attention back to Nick and Jamie. Nick was on his knees raking up piles of jewelry and placing them in the bags. She looked back at the woods where the souls had disappeared. Could she send someone to follow one of those souls to see where they end up? Were they coming back to her world or going to some other dimension? If it was a different dimension, could they get back through here and make it back to our world. Lisa had all these new questions running through her mind as she stood there.

She was looking through the goggles at the town, and it was like it was a new city with clean sidewalks and beautiful buildings. There was too much information and not enough understanding, she thought as she was standing there. Just then, Jamie cleared his throat as he walked up to her and jolted her back into what she was there doing. She hadn't watched Nick gather all the jewelry so she would have to take their word for the fact that he didn't touch any of it.

"Let's go." She said, walking back out onto the street. They walked back the way they had come until they were at the edge of the city. There they waited.

"How much longer are we going to wait?" Nick asked, rubbing the big gloves together that were still on his hands. Lisa looked at Jamie holding his two bags of jewelry. Lisa just looked at him and shook her head. Several minutes later, she saw a portal close enough for them all to make it. Lisa took off, and the other two followed close behind. As they neared the portal, Jamie tripped up and went down on one knee. Nick grabbed one of the suitcases out of his hand. Jamie regained his balance and caught up. They all three pushed through the portal as the soul was coming through. Standing up on the other side of the portal, the first thing Lisa noticed was the deep sand they are standing on. Then, she noticed the sound of ocean waves crashing down. It was the early grey light of morning, just as night was giving way to the day. They all just stood there looking at one another. Were they on an island or a beach area of some county? Lisa thought, standing there looking out at the ocean.

"Now what?" Nick demanded.

"Now we wait." Lisa said calmly as she started walking toward some trees.

"Did either of you touch the stuff with your bare hands?" Lisa asked, staring directly at Nick.

"No, I didn't." Nick said as he stripped off the gloves and threw them to the ground.

"I didn't touch any of it." Jamie said, plopping down beside one of the bags of jewelry. Nick just shook his head as he sat down on the sand. Lisa knew they would be there for a few days, as MaryBeth would need that time to track them down and find a way to get to them. Lisa's cell phone had no service, so she couldn't see where they were or reach out to anyone. There was a big rock that stuck up above the rest of the beach area. Lisa walked over and started to climb it. At the top, she could see the other side of the small island where they landed. She climbed back down the rock and walked back over to where she had left Nick and Jamie.

"It's going to take a few days for them to locate us with the air tags in my bag, and maybe more to get to us." Lisa said. Nick and Jamie just shook their heads and started gathering up water containers from the trash that had washed up, so they could catch rainwater if it came. Lisa began gathering coconuts and stacked them up in the shade. Lisa noticed Nick and Jamie whispering as they were carrying water containers and gathering firewood. Lisa asked Jamie if he was sure they had not touched the stuff on the other side. He assured her they did not. The day was long and hot, and as night fell, Lisa's temper had grown short, and they weren't talking at all. As darkness came on, Nick built a fire, and they settled in to sleep by the fire for the night. Sometime around midnight, Lisa was startled by Nick standing over her. He reached down and pulled her up by the arm. Nick spun her around, and Jamie began to tie her hands behind her back. Before she really knew what was happening, she was tied up.

"What are you doing?" Lisa yelled.

"Well, this is dangerous work, and it's unfortunate that Lisa didn't make it back." Nick said to Jamie with a smile on his face.

"Looks like we get all the jewelry and all the money." Nick said, pushing Lisa down onto the sand. Jamie hunkered down next to Lisa smiling.

"You want to have some fun with her before we drown her." Jamie said with an evil sound to his voice.

Lisa knew she was in trouble, and she had to buy some time till the soul takers came.

"If you kill me, you will be stuck here on the island until they come for you, and you will never get past Bobby and MaryBeth without me." Lisa said, trying not to sound panicky.

"Yea we'd better come up with a better story." Jamie said, standing up to face Nick.

"Besides, we have a couple of days before they can get to us. Let's get some sleep. Nick said as he settled back down onto the sand.

Lisa didn't sleep the rest of the night. Partly because she was scared to close her eyes, and partly because her arms were hurting from her hands being tied behind her back. The next morning, as the night was giving way to the day, Lisa had managed to get herself up in a sitting position. Lisa had twisted her hands hard till her wrists were bleeding, but she got loose from the string Jamie had used to tie her up. She had the gun out of her backpack was going to kill them both. As she sat there waiting for the light of day. Jamie woke up first and stared at her for a long time. Lisa could almost read his thoughts as he stared at her, and it infuriated her. She was about to just shoot him. When Nick rolled over and groaned as he was starting to wake up. Lisa was beginning to believe she had broken the code, and neither one of these guys were going to be taken back over. Sitting there, Lisa was mad at herself for not thinking about the fact that this could happen. She remembered how easily Nick had been convinced to bring one of his buddies instead of Debbie. This must have been his plan all along. Then, there it was, she heard the familiar low rustle of wind in the trees and turned to see who was being taken. Lisa looked over at Nick, and he was trying to speak, but couldn't. She looked at Jamie, and he had fallen back onto the sand. Both men were struggling to move and trying to get up. Then, Lisa could tell their souls were leaving their bodies, as both exhaled their last breath.

Lisa grabbed the goggles from her backpack and looked through the lens. Nick and Jamie's souls looked eerie, being dragged out across the ocean. She looked at Nick's body, and it was lying with one arm slumped on his bag of money. Greedy to the end, she thought. Lisa had watched Nick's body go limp, and she knew he had gone over to the other side. This time, Lisa was so glad they were taken; no, she was glad they were dead. Lisa wondered how Debbie would take the news that her husband was gone, as she sat there quietly.

As the morning wore on, Lisa knew she hadn't figured out how to cross over and take the money without someone dying. It seems that the simple act of taking from the other side is the act that gets you taken to the other side. She pulled Nick's body off the case of jewelry and dragged it into the surf. She pushed it out to sea and went back to get Jamie's body. As she pushed Jamie's body out into the surf and watched it drift away, she was concerned that someone would have to die every time they went over for money. This was something that would have to be accepted by the league and not taken lightly by anyone in the league.

How long before someone gets here? Lisa thought as she stood and poked around in the fire.

I'm sure they are on their way, but I don't know where I am, so I have no idea. Lisa plopped down on the sand, shaking her head at this thought.

Lisa was on that island for nine days before Bobby and his friend came roaring up in a small boat. Lisa was so overjoyed that she ran into Bobby's arms and started sobbing. Bobby swooped her up and carried her to the boat. Bobby's friend grabbed the suitcases and Lisa's backpack. Onboard, she was so relieved, she stretched out on the seat cushions, and she drank all the water Bobby had brought. It took them three hours to get back to the mainland, and Lisa was finished with the ocean and boats. All she wanted was a hot shower, a soft bed and a good night's sleep. She didn't even look back at Bobby as she walked past him and up the stairs to her room in the hotel. As she looked in the mirror at her dirty sunburnt face and stringy twisted hair, she, for the first time, was questioning herself about the whole idea of the league. If Jamie and Nick hadn't decided to wait to come up with a better story, she would be dead. She would have to be more careful and prepared for the ugly human nature of greed. The next morning, as they all ate breakfast, Bobby told Lisa about a new tracker; Nathan had put in the goggles so they could see where she went when she crossed over. He didn't have any more information than the fact that they had put the tracker on her goggles. Lisa was a little upset that she didn't know about it, but was too tired to worry about it. Later that afternoon, they were on the plane and headed for Hendersonville.

Once back in Hendersonville, Lisa knew they had so much information to process that they might spend the rest of their lives figuring it all out. As she walked into the warehouse, she wasn't sure how Debbie would take the loss of her husband. So, when Lisa's eyes met Debbie's eyes, she just shook her head, trying to let Debbie know he was gone.

"He tried to take all the money and had me tied up, so they could drown me. But the soul chasers came and took them both before they could kill me. I guess we'll always need followers. Lisa said, looking at Debbie. Debbie looked sad for just a moment, then raised her head and smiled as she looked at Lisa.

"I guess now I'm with you and the league." Debbie said, looking up at Lisa for assurance.

"I guess so." Lisa said, smiling and nodding her head.

Bobby turned to Nathan and asked if he had been able to track Lisa's location with the new tracker after she crossed over. Nathan shook his head and told the group that as soon as Lisa went through the portal, the tracker lost her, however, as soon as she came back over to this side, it was there again. Lisa had timed herself again with the stopwatch and knew they were in the grave for twenty-three minutes.

"We were in the grave for about twenty-three minutes." Lisa said, holding up her stopwatch.

"How long was the tracker signal gone?" She asked Nathan.

"Let me get my notes." Nathan said as he hurried off to his lab. When he came back, he thumbed through the pages.

"It disappeared at eleven thirty-seven that night and reappeared at ten minutes after four the next morning." Nathan was tracing his notes with his finger as he spoke.

"So, twenty minutes over there is about five hours on this side." MaryBeth said to the group.

"We need to do more testing on all of this." Nathan said, and they all just stood there in the office nodding their heads.

Lisa thanked everyone for coming to get her, then told them all she was taking a couple of days off.

The next night, Lisa felt rested and relaxed and decided to splurge a bit and take her and her team out to a nice restaurant to enjoy some good food and laughter. She made reservations at a ritzy restaurant and texted the time and place to the team. She ordered up an Uber and stepped outside to wait. When the Uber pulled up, she checked the license and the driver, and she gave the little passcode as she climbed in. After a couple of minutes into the drive, the driver took a hard right turn, and her doors locked. What the hell, Lisa thought as she tried the door handle. She called out to the driver, but he just ignored her. She tried getting up to the seat back so she could grab the driver, but he turned the car sharply, throwing her up against the door in the back. Before she could regain herself to try again, they were pulling into a garage. As they pulled in, the door was coming down. The driver stopped the car and jumped out. Three other men opened her door and dragged her out, kicking and punching. They stood her up, and she went to slap one of the men. He simply caught her wrist and pushed it down to her side. The other man put his finger up to his lips and shushed Lisa, which, above all else, just pissed her off. Realizing she was in over her head, she stopped fighting. One of the men grabbed her purse and took her phone out. He turned it off and dropped it into some sort of pouch, then zipped it shut. The men led Lisa up the stairs to a small room and pushed her down into a chair. Two men left, and two men stayed by the door, never taking their eyes off Lisa. In about thirty minutes, a man came in and motioned for Lisa to follow him. Lisa stood and followed. They walked to an exit door and stopped. Well, at least they haven't tied me up or put a bag over my head, Lisa thought as she stood there. Just then, from behind, a canvas bag was slammed over her head and held tightly from behind, pulling her hair. She heard the door open and was being pushed outside. Lisa could hear a helicopter and feel the wind from the propellers. She was roughly lifted and sat in a seat. Someone pulled the strap across her body and clicked it in place.

"Now sit there quietly." A man's voice instructed her. Lisa did as she was told.

Meanwhile, at the restaurant, Bobby, MaryBeth, Nathan and Debbie were waiting for Lisa. After thirty minutes or more, they decided something must have happened, and they all headed back to the warehouse. All of them were thinking about what could've happened.

"Alright, who'd we miss?" Bobby asked. They were all going through their collective perspectives, trying to come up with a solution. Bobby was pacing back and forth. MaryBeth was just sitting behind her desk, staring at her equipment. Nathan was going back through his logs and journals to see if he could find anyone or any link. Debbie knew how money changes people, so she was going through all the contacts from the organizations she had started working with in the last couple of days to see if any of those could have done something.

"Everyone is dead or accounted for." MaryBeth said, shaking her head.

"We have missed something." Bobby spoke as he plopped down in a chair. They sat there pouring over what they had and trying desperately to figure out what they had missed.

On the helicopter, Lisa was acutely aware they had lifted off and were now in the air. It felt like they were flying in circles as the momentum would lean her to the right then to the left. She truly had no idea of where she was. The helicopter stopped moving forward, and she began to feel it going down like the feeling in an elevator as it begins its decent. She felt the thump of them touching down. Suddenly, there were hands on her shoulders as someone unclicked the strap. She was pulled up by her shoulders and forced to the door. There, she was lifted down and out of the helicopter. Once on the ground, she was led away from the helicopter and across the tarmac.

"Stop, wait here." A voice said. Lisa wasn't scared anymore now she was just getting pissed off.

"Step up, you are on stairs." The voice commanded. Lisa detected a Middle Eastern accent in the voice, as her feet and legs started carrying her up the stairs. As she climbed the stairs, she realized she could hear the roar of a plane's engine very loudly. Finally, at the top, someone put his hand on the top of her head and pushed her down as she stepped onto a small jet. Lisa was walked back and shoved down into a seat. She repositioned herself and sat there desperately trying to hear familiar sounds, though there were only the sounds of the plane's engine and the random sound of men's voices, though she was unable to make out anything they were saying.

Back at the warehouse, Bobby was becoming increasingly agitated by not knowing what was going on. He started rifling through the drawers in all the desks.

"Wait a minute." MaryBeth said as she started shuffling through the stacks of paper on her desk.

"Here, here it is! The list of initials and names." She was holding the list up as she spoke. She had found the list early on and had matched every set of initials on it with a police officer, except one. She quickly scanned the page till she found I.I. Those were the initials, and they didn't match anyone's name. MaryBeth had just moved on thinking it was nothing, probably just another bad cop.

"Whose initials are those?" Bobby asked, walking over to MaryBeth.

"I don't know, I couldn't find a match, so I just moved on. We were a little busy at the time." She said sarcastically.

"We need to know who the hell that is." Bobby said, staring at Marybeth. MaryBeth had already started her search. She looked at Bobby with a concerned look, nodded and went back to her computer screens. Debbie started searching the internet, social media and all of the groups she could find, looking for anything. Nathan was still rifling through all of his notes and contacts.

"Found something!" Debbie yelled. Everyone gathered around her computer screen and started reading. I.I. referred to Interactive Investing Group. A firm from the UK. MaryBeth started trying to hack in and see what they were all about as they stood and watched her work.

The small jet had taxied out and had lifted off. Lisa was used to the feeling from all her trips back from wherever she came out of the portal on the small jet. She could feel the plane climbing, then suddenly level off at the cruising altitude. Just as she was feeling the pressure ease off from the climb, a man yanked the bag off her head. The lights of the plane were strong, and she found herself looking away and blinking, trying to get her eyes to focus. When she did get them focused, what she saw scared the hell out of her. There were five men sitting, turned to stare at her. Two looked Middle Eastern, one was oriental, and the other two were English-looking. They all seemed to have contempt for her on their faces. None of them spoke or had much expression to them; they just stared at her. Just then, a man came from behind her and snapped his fingers at the five staring men. They all turned and went about their business, whatever the hell that was. The man sat down across from Lisa and handed her a bottle of water. He smiled at her as she drank thirstily from the plastic bottle. This man was Italian, Lisa thought as she stared at him as angrily as she could.

"Who are you?" Lisa asked after a long drink. The man simply put his finger up to his lips and shushed her again. Lisa turned and stared out the window of the plane into the darkness.

The night wore on back at the warehouse. MaryBeth was searching madly for anything that would give her a clue to how International Investing tied into this. She gave up after a while, not really knowing if or how it was tied to the company. Bobby was going through government agencies to see if he could find a match. Debbie was scrolling through endless lists and feeds; Nathan had given up and was sitting with his hands behind his head. After hours of searching, Bobby stood up and walked outside. MaryBeth followed him and stepped up beside him just outside the door. Bobby was looking up at the night sky, so MaryBeth started looking up too.

"We must find her. We didn't come this far to just lose." Bobby said, never taking his eyes off the night sky.

"Who made the list?" Nathan's question startled them both. Bobby turned and walked back inside.

"Why, what's that got to do with any of this?" Bobby asked as he plopped back down in his chair.

"Because whoever made the list would know what or who I.I. is." MaryBeth said, hurrying back over to her computer. MaryBeth started looking at the list from this angle, and Nathan could see the excitement growing as she changed her searches. Debbie walked over and handed MaryBeth a list of places to investigate that she had come up with. MaryBeth took the list and smiled at Debbie.

As the sun was coming up and beginning to shine in through the small plane's windows, the man who had given Lisa the water earlier reached over and slid the small shade down. They had been in the air for hours, and Lisa's mind was racing, trying to figure out what was going on. Lisa could feel the plane begin its decent and knew she was about to land. Her heart filled with dread as her mind was spinning almost out of control. She didn't know where she was, or who these people were, or why they wanted her. The plane landed, and all the shades were pulled down so Lisa couldn't see anything to give her a clue as to where she was. The man came over to Lisa, holding the bag. Lisa shook her head to let him know she didn't want to go back in there. He held up a blindfold and smiled. Lisa rolled her eyes but nodded. The blindfold would be better than a bag over her head. She stood, and he put the blindfold on her, took her by the arm and led her toward the door. As they stepped out onto the platform, the man whispered trust me, as she stepped down onto the first step. Lisa was expecting heat when she stepped out of the plane, as she was sure they were in the desert. But it was cold here, and not just Tennessee cold but bitterly cold. The air was so cold going into her lungs that she could barely breathe it in. Lisa realized she had absolutely no idea where she was or what was going to happen.

As the sun rose back in Hendersonville, Bobby and MaryBeth were no closer to knowing who or what had taken Lisa. As Marybeth finished one last search of some database, she felt completely beaten.

"What do we have?" Bobby asked.

"Nothing, not a damn thing. We killed everyone associated with this list, remember?" MaryBeth said slamming her pencil down on the desk. Bobby and Nathan just sat there staring at nothing. Debbie was frustrated by all her searches and was sitting slumped in her chair.

"Let's leave it alone for a bit, go get some breakfast. When we get back, we can start again." Bobby said, standing up and grabbing his jacket. The four of them left and headed for a restaurant.

As they drove away, Nathan asked about the tracker MaryBeth had put on Lisa's phone. MaryBeth shook her head and said someone had turned it off.

"Who would do that?" Nathan asked.

"Not sure, but I can't see her or reach her with any messages. It's like her phone has just disappeared." MaryBeth said as she clicked her seatbelt on. When they reached the restaurant, they weren't really talking or in the mood to talk. So, they sat quietly and ate their food without much discussion of anything. Each one was going through everything over and over in their heads.

Lisa was led across the tarmac, and she was trying desperately to figure out where they could be that was so cold. Antarctica, Iceland, perhaps the Arctic Circle, she thought with a smile. The man led her into a building with warmth. Lisa was chilled to the bone and had begun to shiver. She felt a man's jacket being slipped over her shoulders.

Lisa nodded her head as she needed to prepare for whatever she faced when they took the blindfold off. She could tell they were back inside by the temperature and the fact that the wind had stopped blowing. They made their way through another door, and she could tell by the sounds of their feet that they were in a hallway of some sort. They stopped while she heard a door being unlocked, she guessed from the inside. She was led through the door and seated in a hard-bottom chair.

"You may remove your blindfold." A British voice calmly told her. She took the blindfold off and was surprised to see only one man sitting in a chair directly in front of her. Lisa looked around the room searching for anything that could give her a clue as to her whereabouts. There was nothing, just bare walls. The man sitting in front of her smiled and raised his hands as if to say relax.

"Do you know who I am, or where you are?" the man asked, staring straight into Lisa's eyes.

"No, I don't have any idea of anything right now." Lisa spoke as calmly as she could. The man took a deep breath through his nose and exhaled. He nodded as he stood up.

"First, let me apologize for the way you have been treated. It is crude, but we must maintain complete isolation and stay invisible to the rest of the world." The man spoke very easily. Lisa wondered about his accent, maybe English or Australian, but he was trying to conceal it. Lisa was sure of it.

"We represent a very powerful world organization. We work to protect the people of this earth, and to protect the earth itself. I won't bore you with the details of what exactly we do, but we will do whatever is necessary to carry out our mission. Our organization controls many governments around the world. War and peace turn on our decisions and actions. You have now entered the world stage with your league, and now it's time for you to decide the future for yourself and the league." The man had turned away from Lisa as he spoke, and when he finished speaking, he turned his head to look at Lisa. Lisa sat and stared at the man; she wasn't sure what would happen if she told him about all the money or the fact that they would continue collecting the money. She didn't know what to say, so she just sat there shivering.

"We know about the lens and souls, the crossing over and coming back, though we can never pinpoint where you will be returning. We've seen the jewelry and all the money. What we don't know but certainly need to know is your intentions." The man came back over and sat down in front of Lisa. He sat back and smiled at her. Lisa still wasn't sure about all of this, but she knew she had to say something, so she took a deep breath and began,

"We have all the things you know about, the lens, the crossover with followers, the return, which, by the way we can't pinpoint either. The bags were stuffed full of jewelry and precious stones. Yes, we sell them and collect the money. The members of the league have sworn an oath to use the money to benefit the earth and help people we have written out some strategies that we believe will let us do that. If you kill me, it all stops. The league goes into hiding, and you will never hear from them again." Lisa was speaking faster than she was thinking and her emotions were taking over. The man just sat there quietly with his arms folded smiling at Lisa. They just stared at one another for several seconds.

"Walk with me." The man said, standing up. As they walked down the corridor, Lisa could see through open doors into busy rooms. There seemed to be so many people working with a purpose. Lisa turned to look behind her. All seven of the men who brought her here were walking behind them. The man led her into a large room with giant screens showing maps of the world on some and neighborhood streets on others. Lisa just stood there trying to take in everything.

"We have no desire to kill you or even stop the league. But we must make certain that anyone who enters the world stage has no intention of harming the world. We believe you and your league will do the right things and use the money for good causes. We were watching as you took down the company. We cleared the bodies from Mr. McDavid's house, and you will find it cleaned and ready for you when you return. We believe you intend to do good with all of this power. However, there are many forces in the world that will try to take power from you and use it for their own gain. We believe that was Henry McDavid's purpose, to stuff his own pockets and hurt anyone who got in his way, and even try to rule the world. So, when the league took him, and the company out then started pouring the money into the future of the world. Yes, we knew then." As the man finished speaking, Lisa began to see what was going on. They were monitoring the entire world, and if what the man told her is true, manipulating it and its people.

"We are the International Independence Organization, and we work silently to ensure each country has its interests met and its people have the chance to grow and prosper. The man snapped his fingers and pointed to a screen. The scene on the screen changed, and Lisa was looking at the warehouse. She saw Bobby pacing back and forth inside the warehouse. We will work for you in the shadows. As long as you do the right things, we will open doors for you that you never knew you needed open. We will find ways to connect you and the league to people and organizations that can help you on this journey. You will only know we're there if you start in a different direction. In that case, we will close all the doors, and when we have you closed in, we will end you and the league. If you find you are under threat, we will help neutralize the threat. We ask nothing from you. Just follow your mission and do what you say you are going to do with this money and power. Know that we are always watching." The man finished talking and walked over to the door. The door was open, and he stepped into the doorway; he stopped and turned to look at Lisa. He smiled, stepped out and was gone. The other man stepped into the doorway and motioned for Lisa to follow him. They walked in silence to the end of the corridor, where the man turned and, with the blind fold and, motioned for Lisa to come to him.

"Can a girl get a sandwich for Pete's sake?" Lisa said as she stepped up to the man. They stood there at the door waiting. Lisa heard the small plane's engine as it pulled up on the tarmac. Lisa was led out of the building and back across the tarmac through the cold and onto the plane, where she was seated and told she could take the blindfold off. When she took it off, there was a man standing there with a tuna fish sandwich. Lisa knew she had nothing to worry about as she took the sandwich.

Meanwhile, back in Hendersonville Bobby, MaryBeth, Debbie, and Nathan had come back to the warehouse. Bobby was pacing back and forth while the rest were sitting just staring at one another.

"Maybe she just left to figure some things out for herself." Nathan said as he fiddled with a rubrics cube. Bobby and Marybeth just looked at him, they knew they didn't have anything else to go on. Debbie had already started searching again and was looking at her screens. Bobby decided to get up and start moving the money from the back and preparing it for deposits. MaryBeth started building platforms to funnel the money into the different agencies and scientific programs as grants. Nathan went back to his lab and started working on his experiments. The morning seemed to drag on into the afternoon, and each of them could barely work. They found themselves sitting around Lisa's desk, trying desperately to come up with any shred of an idea.

As the small plane landed, Lisa overheard one of the pilots say Atlanta. At least we're in the United States, she thought with a smile. Lisa had to put the blindfold back on and was led down the stairs from the plane and across the tarmac. She was led inside the building and down a hallway. They led her into a room where she was seated and told to sit still until someone came for her. Lisa sat there for several minutes waiting for someone, anyone's voice. After several minutes, she raised her head up to peek out through the bottom of her blindfold. As she looked around, she realized there were no voices or any sounds for that matter. She slowly took the blindfold off and looked around. Lisa sat there smiling for a minute, wondering how long she had sat there by herself. The ding of her phone startled her, and she jumped in her chair. Her phone just kept dinging with all the messages MaryBeth had sent her. She slowly raised the phone and hit the button to call MaryBeth. Lisa told MaryBeth she was in Atlanta and would explain everything when she got back. She hung up the phone and sat there trying to make sense of what she had just been through. She came out of the small room and walked into the main corridor leading to the ticket counter. A smile came across her face as she walked because she knew the league was on the right track. Two hours later, she was on a plane to Nashville. As she sat there, she was thinking about how easily they had gotten to her and how powerless she was with them.

When Debbie picked her up in Nashville, Lisa didn't have much to say, so they rode back to the warehouse in silence. Lisa came walking in with a smile on her face, shaking her head. MaryBeth ran over and hugged her, squeezing her tightly.

"Have a nice trip?" Bobby asked in a smart-ass tone. Lisa sat down and told them all she knew. Which, when she said it all out loud, wasn't that much. It all came down to doing what they said they were going to do. When Lisa told them the name of the organization, International Independence, all three of them let out a moan of recognition. MaryBeth grabbed her list and showed Lisa the initials they had been trying to find.

"They must've been on to us for a while, that's why they let us take Henry and the company out." Lisa said.

"We all have our jobs to do so tomorrow let's get in here and start changing the world." Lisa finished talking and stood up. She walked over and hugged everyone, even Bobby's friend, who was just sitting and listening. Lisa left the warehouse and headed home.

That evening, she sat down at Henry's old lake house, her new home with Tim's journal. She sat for several minutes staring blankly out over the Cumberland River. Lisa slowly turned to a new page in the journal and wrote a new entry.

I know we will figure all this out, and as long as we use this power for good, we are on the right track. As long as we have followers, we can help save the world.

Lisa closed the journal and sat back, smiling and breathing in the night air.

CHAPTER XIII
The League

Eleven months had passed since the league had taken over the company. Lisa was in charge as the president of the company. Bobby was the safety and security director. MaryBeth oversaw accounting and budget, and Debbie was covering where the league was investing its time and money organizations, social media, things like that. Nathan was overseeing research and development, and his lab was working on all kinds of things. The entire business had become like a nine-to-five job for each of them, they had hired several employees, and everything was going along quite well. No one had crossed over for the entire eleven months. Lisa was struggling with the whole follower thing and the knowledge that when someone followed them over, they would lose their life. The fact was, though, if they wanted to use this new power for good, they would need money, and that meant crossing over, and with that, followers would lose their lives.

Lisa was learning she couldn't be in charge of the league and all its operations; she had to leave a lot of it to the team. She was in the warehouse every day, working to find ways to use the money for the good of the planet and the people on the planet. She had a good team working with her, and they all had their parts to do and were doing them all very well. In the months since the takeover, she had decided to keep the house in Sarasota as a getaway. She had cleared the title to Henry's river house and had taken ownership of it. The league was working hard to make a positive impact on the world stage.

Lisa was growing restless, though and wanted to crossover soon, though she was no closer to understanding the grave than she was eleven months ago. They had calculated the time spent on the other side and what it meant in this world's time. Maybe when she started crossing again, they could even calculate where she might turn up when she crosses back over, unless of course, the portals were just random based on where the souls died in this world. The one thing she really wanted to solve was the fact that when a follower went over and gathered and carried back the jewels and stones, they would be taken back over for eternity. Without solving this, someone would have to die, according to what death is in this world, each time they crossed. Lisa had to reckon with this. Was the cost of a life worth all the good they were doing in the world? Lisa carried this weight; this was on her to reconcile. Her team carried all the good things the league had to offer; Lisa would carry this part. Her next time over would be with two people again, one would gather the jewels and fill the cases. The other one would carry them back across. Lisa needed to define what got people taken back over.

She sat on the porch in the evening, looking out over the Cumberland River and was thinking through this whole process. It seemed that the person who gathered the jewels was taken back but they had also always carried the jewels back across the portal too. So, she would need someone to gather the jewelry and fill the cases, but not carry it back across the portal. And someone to not touch the jewelry on the other side and carry them back across the portal. The second person could stand at the edge of the woods and not even enter the town or the building. They would just carry the bags of stuff back across the portal. Lisa sat there thinking about the whole process of gathering up the stuff and carrying it back through. Tim had gathered and carried, as had most of the others. Nick gathered, and Jamie just carried, yet they both were taken back. That didn't make sense unless Nick took one of the bags as they came back over. Lisa closed her eyes and pictured them coming back through onto that island. When she stopped and regained her balance, Nick was holding one of the cases. Had he carried it through, she thought. She had been focused on Jamie not touching the jewelry, she had missed that Nick had carried one of the bags back over.

"Nick carried one of the bags through the portal." Lisa said under her breath. Lisa sat there with her mind spinning on a thought. In that moment of thought, Lisa realized she might have figured something out.

"What if carrying the bags back through the portal is what does it. What if they don't carry the bags back across the portal? What if they throw it through the portal and then just come through empty-handed like me?" Lisa said aloud.

That might just work, she thought. Lisa decided to get a couple of people and crossover soon.

Lisa decided to recruit two people and not a couple this time. One of the two can load up the two suitcases and get them ready. The other person could carry the bags, but not through the portal. We will throw them through the portal, she thought. As she finished her whiskey and got ready for bed, she was getting excited over this possible breakthrough. As she was lying down to sleep, her mind was running through the fact that she didn't know what would happen if they threw the bags through. Would they come out on the other side with them? Would they be lost forever? She didn't know, but now she really wanted to find out.

The next day in the office, Lisa was figuring out how to get two followers, the old you're my boyfriend, so follow me may not work here. She decided that until she knew for sure how this new theory worked or didn't work, she would need to keep any followers she found away from the league. So, for now, the new boyfriend story was all she had. Lisa told Bobby and Nathan about her plan and what she wanted to try. Nathan thought it was a good idea and was truly curious about not carrying the stuff through the portal. He seemed more curious about whether it would come out on the other side of the portal.

"That could be the secret to this crossover piece." Nathan said as he walked away. He set off to start calculating to see if he could answer his question.

Lisa and MaryBeth went to a local restaurant for lunch, and while they were sitting there, Lisa noticed a man sitting by himself. Lisa had explained her theory to MaryBeth, and MaryBeth agreed it could work.

"I wonder how I can get that guy to notice me?" Lisa asked MaryBeth. MaryBeth just turned to the man and said, "Hey you, come over here." Lisa looked at MaryBeth, shaking her head and rolling her eyes.

"Hi, I'm MaryBeth, and this is Lisa, and Lisa here thinks you are quite handsome." MaryBeth chuckled as she stood to leave.

"I'll leave you two alone here to work out the details. Lisa, I'll see you back at the office." MaryBeth finished talking, spun around and was gone in an instant.

Lisa was left just staring at this young man, standing at her table, waiting for him to introduce himself. The man just stood there and smiled at Lisa. Lisa motioned for the man to sit down, and he did.

"So, I'm Lisa, and you are? Lisa said, sticking her hand out across the table to shake his.

"I know who you are." The man said.

"You run the league, giving all that money to charities and organizations to help the planet and its people, right?" The man said, still not shaking Lisa's hand. Lisa was taken aback and stared at the man.

"Yes, that's me." Lisa said, pulling her hand back.

"You have a very exclusive club there in the league. Lots of people are noticing what you're doing, and lots of questions are being asked about how you're doing it." The man spoke with strong confidence.

"You a reporter?" Lisa asked in a frustrated tone.

"Yes, freelance as it is, and I've been looking into the league for a bit now. Would you like to grant me an exclusive interview and tour of the facility to answer my questions?" The man asked, now smiling.

"Yes, I will, but not today. Give me a number where I can reach you, and soon, I will sit down and answer all your questions. Lisa spoke as her mind was racing through what all this meant. The man wrote a phone number on a piece of napkin and stood to leave.

"What's your name?" Lisa asked.

"Colsen, Tate." The man said as he walked away.

When Lisa got back to the warehouse, she told everyone about Colsen. She told them all to keep their eyes open for anyone following them or poking around inside the compound. She reminded them that the things they have and the power they wield would destroy the world if it got out. They all stood there looking at one another, nodding in agreement. Bobby told everyone to double-check their security protocols and make sure no one can get into the league. He set off to get his team to up the security around the warehouse. Lisa left for the day and went to a bar to get a drink and find a follower. She had sat at the bar for a while when she noticed Colsen sitting at a small table in the corner. Lisa took her drink, walked over and sat down. She was irritated because obviously Colsen had been following her, and she hadn't noticed. Lisa decided to see if Colsen was up for an adventure, she was going to see if he wanted to cross over with her. If her theory was correct, she would be adding another person to her team, maybe with connections to folks she wouldn't have. If her theory is wrong, well, one less reporter to worry about.

"You up for an adventure?" Lisa asked, leaning forward. Colsen just looked at her, waiting for the rest of the story. Lisa set about telling him about the crossover and the jewelry and the thrill of it all. Colsen smiled, nodded and pulled out forty dollars to cover their tab. The two of them left with a purpose and walked to Lisa's car. Colsen left his car in the parking lot and rode with Lisa to the warehouse.

When Lisa and Colsen came walking in, MaryBeth and Debbie stopped what they were doing and stared.

"We're crossing over tonight." Lisa announced as she started to gather up her stuff. Bobby had already left for the day, and both MaryBeth and Debbie were getting ready to leave.

"Have you talked to Bobby about this?" Debbie asked firmly.

"I don't need to talk to Bobby, nor do I need his permission." Lisa said while she was getting her backpack ready. MaryBeth walked up to Lisa and turned her back on Colsen so she could speak to Lisa without Colsen seeing what she was saying.

"Lisa, who is this guy, and what the hell are you doing?" MaryBeth asked her questions with a big smile on her face.

Lisa stopped what she was doing and looked at both MaryBeth and Debbie.

"Ladies, this is Colsen, Colsen Tate, and we have hit it off so I'm going to crossover with him tonight. Now, please stop asking questions and help me get ready." Lisa was staring at MaryBeth in a way that made MaryBeth nervous. Lisa's phone dinged, and she glanced at it. It was Bobby texting her. She looked at Debbie, who was holding her phone, and shook her head, Debbie just smiled back.

MaryBeth went to the back and brought her two carry-on bags. Lisa took one and left the other. She was trying an experiment tonight, and having only one bag would make it easier. Lisa double checked her backpack, and she and Colsen headed for the door. Lisa called an Uber, and they waited. Colsen had not said a word since they left the bar. When they got out of the car at the little church down the road from the crossover spot, Lisa couldn't take it anymore.

"Colsen, are you really ok with this?" Lisa asked sternly.

"Yes, I'm just paying close attention, so I don't miss anything. I don't think I'll have time to take notes," Colsen said as they started walking down the lonely back road.

"It's easy, just follow me, and don't hesitate when the time comes to cross over." Lisa went on to explain what they were going to be doing. "We will follow a soul that I can see through my special lenses. We'll follow it to a blue portal sphere, that's where we will cross. We go through just before the soul gets there. We will come out on the other side of the portal in our graves, so you may see different things than I see. We are still trying to figure that out. You will gather up jewelry that is strewn all around on the ground. Then we find another portal, where a soul is coming through, and you will throw the bag full of stuff through, and we come back through to our side of the grave." When Lisa finished, she looked at Colsen, and he was looking very distrustful at that moment.

"So, I just blindly follow you through a portal to another dimension where I gather up jewelry and stuff from the grave and bring them back?" Colsen asked with a level of uncertainty in his voice. They had stopped at the spot and were waiting for a soul.

"Yes." That was all Lisa said.

"Call me Cole, only my mom calls me Colsen." Colsen said. Lisa just smiled at him.

"When we're done with this little adventure, you will give me that exclusive interview and tour, right?" Cole asked.

"Yes, of course that was our deal." Lisa said, smiling.

After a few minutes, Lisa heard the familiar sound of the wind rustling through the trees. She started looking around in all directions until she saw the soul of a woman coming out of the woods behind them.

"Here we go." Lisa said as she handed the lenses to Cole and pointed to where he should look.

"Holy Crap!" was all Cole could say as he handed the lenses back to Lisa. Lisa put the goggles on and took off after the soul. Cole was just trying to keep up with her. Deep in the woods, Lisa saw the portal and told Cole to keep up as she sped up and went past the soul. Lisa grabbed Cole as she went through, pulling him through with her. On the other side, they stopped and stood there for a moment. Lisa was reconditioning herself with the sights and smells, and Cole was trying his best to understand what he was looking at.

"Let's go." Lisa said as they headed off in the direction they had just come from.

"Oh my god. I thought this was just some sort of test or prank you were playing to make me dance for the interview. But we are in some other dimension, right?" Cole was speaking nervously.

"That's right, you my friend are inside your own grave." Lisa said as they walked. This information sent a shiver down Cole's back, and he got just a little closer to Lisa as they walked. In only a couple of minutes or so, they were on the streets of a decaying city, and Lisa was looking for a building to go into. The two walked past a few buildings with the doors all closed, so when the next one came up. A very large building. Lisa walked up to the door and kicked it. It took two kicks, but the door gave way, and they walked inside. Lisa instructed Cole to fill the carry-on as quickly as he could while she kept watch. Cole set about doing what he was told. Lisa was standing at the door watching the souls wandering around, walking back and forth. After a few minutes, Cole announced he was ready, and the two of them walked back out onto the street. They walked for a bit until they came to the edge of town. There they stood and waited. Lisa reminded Cole not to touch the bag inside the portal. They must throw it through and follow it, and they only have a few seconds to get through before the portal closes. As they stood there, Lisa was wondering if she had broken the code, and this would allow her to cross over without some poor unsuspecting person dying. Finally, a blue sphere appeared close enough for them to get to, and they were off. Lisa was pointing and showing Cole where to throw the bag. Cole ran up and swung the carry-on bag through into the portal as hard as he could. Lisa ran by him and into the portal, and Cole took a quick glance back as he felt Lisa yank him through the portal. When he came out the other side, they were standing on a hill in some trees. Lisa was looking all around in the dark for the carry-on bag to make sure it had come through. Then, there it was just lying there just a few feet from them. Lisa took her phone out, that's when she noticed Cole was just standing there staring into space.

"You alright?" Lisa asked.

"Yes, I'm fine, I just don't understand what we just did." Cole said, shaking his head.

Lisa was searching for their location on her phone. Luckily, being on top of the hill allowed her phone to work. Though she wasn't sure about what it was telling her.

"Nunavut Canada." She said, sounding sarcastic. Lisa texted MaryBeth to say they were back. MaryBeth responded very quickly and said she was working on getting to them. Head southeast toward Rankin Inlet was the last text message she got, so they headed off in that direction. The terrain was thick and wet with large piles of trees down, and the mud was knee deep in places. The going was very difficult, and the fact that they didn't know where exactly they were going made it even more difficult. Finally, just before the light of day, they found a road. It was a dirt road, no it was a path through a field, but Lisa was calling it a road. They kept on heading southeast toward Rankin Inlet. They walked most of the next day without seeing a single car or person on the road they were on. Finally, at last Lisa could see the tops of buildings and smell the smells of civilization, they had made it to Rankin Inlet. It was late in the afternoon, and suddenly Lisa realized that at any moment they could be coming for Cole. She started looking around for a place to hide, just in case. There were no hotels in Rankin Inlet; the one store in the village had an owner who said he had a room they could share for the night for a small amount. Lisa took him up on his offer quickly and rushed off to the room, fearing the soul chasers might be coming at any moment. The two of them retired to a small, smelly room to crash for the night. As the sun went down and the few house lights came on around the village, Lisa grew uneasy, almost nervous. She was still waiting to hear the low rustling sound of the wind in the trees and watch helplessly as Cole was taken back.

"I have to eat." Cole's voice startled Lisa, and she jumped.

"Yes, I'm hungry too." Lisa said. Lisa grabbed her backpack and told Cole to leave the suitcase as they headed out to find something to eat. As they walked down the street back to the small store where they had found the room, Lisa was on high alert. She figured if she heard the low rustle, she could move Samuel off to the side of the road and hide him. They reached the store, and Lisa was beginning to think maybe she had found a way to bring everyone back. The store had cans of soup, so they bought some soup, crackers and water. As they walked back to the shack where they were staying, Lisa felt Cole glaring at her.

They got back, and as they heated up their soup, Lisa was trying to remember the longest anyone had made it back over on this side. Had Cole made it? Was he going to be alright? Lisa thought, sitting there staring off into space.

"What is wrong?" Cole asked, almost demanding an answer.

"Nothing, nothing at all." Lisa said, snapping back into the moment and taking her soup from Cole.

The night was cold and long for both of them, and neither really slept much. The next morning, as the sun rose, Lisa felt a wave of relief, and she watched Cole climb out of bed. That's it, we have figured it out. It's the portal she thought, neither side matters, it's about what you bring back through the portal.

Lisa got a text from MaryBeth saying their plane would be there in the afternoon if the weather held, but that didn't look promising. Lisa decided to tell Cole about what had just happened. She hoped he would understand.

They sat quietly in front of the fireplace, trying to get warm. Lisa looked at Cole, smiled and started telling him about the league and what they were trying to do. Before she told him anything else she decided she needed his reaction to being a guinea pig for them.

"Look, here's the deal. When we crossed over, you were a follower just like all the other followers that have gone across with me. You carry the bag, gather the stuff and carry it back. The difference this time was that I had an idea about how to keep you alive." Lisa paused to see Cole's reaction so far.

"Wait, what do you mean, keep me alive?" Cole asked, squinting his eyes at Lisa.

"When the followers come back through carrying the bags, they were doomed. The next day, the other side would send soul takers to take the follower's soul back. I figured out that it was the act of carrying the bag back across the portal that caused this. That's why I had you throw the bag through the portal and not touch it in the portal. It worked; you're still here." Lisa was smiling as she finished.

Cole just sat there staring at Lisa, processing everything he had just been told.

"When you say, you had figured it out, it was just a theory, right? You didn't really know if it was going to work or not, did you? I was your test case, your guinea pig." Cole was starting to get upset as he spoke, Lisa could hear it in his voice.

"That's true." Lisa said looking down into the fire.

"But understand we have a great scientist in the league, and he was almost certain it was going to work." Lisa finished talking and looked straight at Cole.

"Almost certain, that was good enough for you to risk my life. You put my life in danger, you bitch, you knew I could have died. You, you were testing a theory with my life." Cole had stood up and was very angry as he spoke. Lisa just sat and stared at the fire, not sure what to say to this. She had hoped Cole would understand and would want to join the league, but now she's not sure of what he is going to do. Cole grabbed Lisa up by the collar and pulled her up to him.

"What made you think this would work? At least tell me you had a fair amount of evidence to back your stupid theory." Cole said, pushing Lisa away and flopping back down in his chair. Lisa raised her head and looked deeply at Cole, then she began speaking slowly.

"I know it was a shitty thing to do, but you would never have gone if I had told you the whole thing, and we needed to move on this as soon as we could. We didn't really have time to find a follower and get them to trust me and follow me, which takes weeks. Frankly, I want you in the league. We need someone like you who can help us get the true word out about what we're doing. Help us get to governments across the world so we can help the people of Earth. We were ninety-nine percent sure we had figured it out, and now that we know it for sure, it opens up a whole new channel. Besides, you were up for it, you were willing to follow me into an unknown world, dimension, whatever the hell it is, just for money and an interview. So, you had to know there was a risk." Lisa was almost pleading with Cole as she explained what she had done. Cole walked over and opened the carry-on bag. It was still packed full of all the jewelry he had gathered. He picked up a couple of rings and looked at them in the light.

"So, this is where you are getting your funds right? You go over and gather up this stuff from over there and bring it back to what, sell it, melt it down, what?" Cole spoke as he was picking through the jewelry.

"We do both, now. Sell some and melt some. It depends on what it is and what we're trying to do." Lisa said, looking at Cole.

"I'll need all the details of what the other side is and what you are doing, when you're doing it, where, who, you know, the whole story. I want to be a part of this. I want to be in the league, and now I believe I've earned it." Cole threw the rings back into the carry-on and zipped it up. Lisa turned back toward the fire and nodded.

There was a storm coming in, so they both knew they would be there at least another day. They ended up at the store owner's house with his wife making dinner for them and listening to the history of Rankin Inlet. After dinner, they walked back to their shack and began settling in for the night. Lisa was watching Cole as he was stoking the fire. She hadn't noticed before just how muscular he was. She hadn't noticed his strong eyes and dark hair. As they sat in front of the fire, Lisa became aware of Cole looking at her. She had been aware of the tension that was between them all day and wasn't sure how to break it. She looked up at Cole, and their eyes met.

"I was freezing last night." Cole said smiling.

"Me too." Lisa said.

"Maybe we should sleep together tonight, you know, for the body heat." Cole suggested. Later that night, they crawled into the bed together and snuggled up to stay warm. Somewhere in the night, they made love to one another and became very close. The next morning, when Lisa woke, Cole was sitting by the fireplace with a cup of coffee. Lisa got dressed and joined him. The storm had passed, and Lisa got a text from MaryBeth telling her the plane was on its way. Lisa responded to her text with a thumbs-up. Then she sent another text telling her that the theory of not carrying things back through the portal had worked as they all knew it would. She added a winky face emoji and told her Cole was with her. Once they were on the plane heading back to civilization, Cole looked over at Lisa and smiled.

"Don't ever lie to me or not tell me the whole truth again." That was your one pass. If it ever happens again, I'll blow the league and you apart, understand." Cole said, staring at Lisa. Lisa smiled and nodded because she knew she had not only found a great addition to the league, but to her life as well.

For the rest of her days, Lisa worked tirelessly to understand what the portals meant and what was on the other side. She worked to better the world she lived in using the league. She eventually married Cole, and they had three great kids. Two of them would be carrying on the league's mission and work. Her eldest son was in politics and would help the league from a senator's seat. The others worked every day to make the world a better place, while they waited their turn to be taken to the grave and beyond.

Lisa left the warehouse and headed home for the last time. Her children would carry the league now. That evening, she sat down at Henry's old lake house, the house she and Cole had lived in before he passed away, the home where she had raised her children. She sat down on the back porch with Tim's journal. She sat for several minutes staring blankly out over the Cumberland River. Lisa slowly turned to her last entry in the journal and wrote.

I know they will continue to figure all this out, and as long as they use this power for good, they will continue to make the world a better place. They can keep it going and maybe, just maybe, save the world on this side of the grave.

Lisa closed the journal and sat back, smiling and looking into the darkness of the night.